WARNING

This book contains sexually explicit scenes and adult language. It may be considered offensive to some readers. This book is for sale to adults ONLY.

* * * * * * * * * * * * * * * * *

Please store your files wisely where they cannot be accessed by underage readers.

ISBN-13: 978-1988083971
ISBN-10: 1988083974

Other Books by Darla Dunbar:

<u>The Romeo Alpha BBW Paranormal Shifter Romance Series</u> (This series precedes the "<u>Romeo Alpha Blood Lines Romance Series</u>")

Amanda Walker thinks that she has a normal and boring life. That is until after her 24th birthday. Everything changes when she meets the man who says he was supposed to be her husband. Denying everything the man says, she fights him every step of the way. But after he kidnaps her, Amanda discovers that there are some things about her family that her parents kept a secret all these years. Among the history of the family she learns secrets she thought only happened in story books. Can Amanda tell the difference between truth and lies or is she this mysterious woman that holds the key to a legacy?

<u>The Alpha Feud BBW Paranormal Shifter Romance Series</u>

Eliza's life consisted of reporting on boring, crowd-pleasing events, like their country livestock fair. With the arrival of two handsome brothers, the lives of Eliza and her best friend, Melissa, are shaken to the core. For Eliza, the arrival of this new man becomes a test of her relationship with her current boyfriend, who she's been happily living with for over six years. Does Hayden, a complete stranger, really wield the power to make Eliza reconsider her relationship with Andrew?

The Alpha Packed BBW Paranormal Shifter Romance Series

Darlene has led a quiet life since suffering through a terrible break-up. She wants nothing more than to spend her time in front of the TV, away from any sort of trouble. But all that goes down the drain when handsome, rugged and rough Idris comes into her life. He is a werewolf on the lookout for his missing pack leader. Darlene quickly finds herself pulled towards this mysterious man and at the same time finds herself falling deeper and deeper into the world of the supernatural.

The Daemon Paranormal Romance Chronicles

The daemon infighting can only be stopped when a strong leader emerges to calm the different factions. Juno appears to be at the heart of the conflict. Things become complicated when Phoebe and Supay try to negotiate with the siren, Juno. The love triangle among Phoebe, Supay and Apollo become tense when Juno's meddling threatens to destroy any romance that develops.

The Mind Talker Paranormal Romance Series

Ananda finds herself on the run and she's not alone. With help from Jared, a stranger that she just met, the two evade capture by an organization that is intent on hunting her kind. Ananda and Jared are able to read minds. When an unfortunate incident happened involving a disturbed individual that resulted in the death of his schoolmates, the secret organization decided to take action.

<u>The Leather Satchel Paranormal Romance Series</u>

Valtina is stuck in Middle World, unable to pass on to The Afterlife. In order to redeem herself from past deeds done, she must help bring romance back into the world and stop The Dark Side from destroying love in its entirety. Following orders issued by Ladaya and armed with a leather satchel filled with the appropriate tools and weapons, Valtina embraces each mission with enthusiasm.

Get the latest update on new releases from the author at:

https://darladunbar.com/newsletter/

This book is Part Four of the "<u>Romeo Alpha Blood Lines Romance Series</u>" and follows twenty-four years after "<u>The Romeo Alpha BBW Paranormal Shifter Romance Series</u>"

1 - Blood Lines

Twenty-four years have passed in relative peace for Amanda and Romeo. They've raised five children into adulthood and are thoroughly enjoying their lives as the Alpha King and Queen of the werewolves. At twenty-four, Sarina is just stepping into her powers and will be ripe for mating when her birthday comes in two weeks. What no one knows is the danger that lurks just outside their tight knit community. Romeo has made peace with the other clans and has enjoyed that peace, but it will all come crashing down around him when his oldest daughter comes of age to take a mate.

2 - Alpha Infiltration

Brody is an attentive and loving mate and Sarina finds herself engulfed by the love of her family. When things start to change with the twins though, Sarina finds herself torn in two. She loves Brody in a way she's never loved another man, human or wolf. When he shows signs of the dark void, however, she can't decide whether to run from him or to him. She's frightened for both of her sons and struggles with her own mortality.

3 - Alpha Bait

Lilith is on the loose, plotting and planning with Fenris to take down the Delta pack and its alpha, Romeo. Sarina and Brody have their work cut out for them in order to stop the hostile takeover. With their wedding on the horizon, both feel compelled to spend time with their family even as danger lurks around every corner. When the twin babies, Jedidiah and Brody Jr., go missing, all hands are on deck to search for the leaders of the next generation of the Delta pack. And as Sarina and Brody dig deeper into Lilith's past, especially where Romeo is concerned, they find a mind twisted by deception and an overly unhealthy obsession with power.

4 - Alpha Strategy

With Lilith's soul separated from her body, Romeo and Amanda are bent on seeing her body destroyed so that she never comes back again. What they've forgotten in the meantime is that Lilith wasn't alone in her desire over control of the Delta pack and Romeo. Sarina and Brody are finally enjoying a quiet life, not that they expect it to last long. Their wedding, a source of great stress, is just weeks away. With all that's going on though, Sarina wonders if she'll ever be able to legally wed her mate.

5 - Alpha Revelation

Lilith has haunted the Traverse family since the beginning but her obsession with the reigning alpha and his immediate family is more than Romeo's eldest daughter can stand. In a twisted allegiance with her first mate, Fenris, Lilith has caused unbearable pain to the Delta pack's community and now she has gone as far as to make a deal with the Devil. She has comfortably inhabited Sarina's body, playing wife to Brody and mother to the couple's twin boys. Digging her way up from Hell wasn't easy, but Sarina harnesses powers that rival even those of her mother.

Alpha Romeo Blood Lines Romance Series

Alpha Revelation

Book Five

By Darla Dunbar

Copyright Revelry Publishing 2016

Table of Contents

Chapter One

"**WE'VE GOT** some serious decisions to make," Amanda said, chuckling when Romeo rolled his eyes. Deep down, she felt uneasy proceeding with the wedding while everything was still in turmoil but for now, she had to play along. "Well, it's not every day you give away our eldest daughter you know."

"Seems to me I did that a while back when she mated that little whelp," said Romeo, joking.

"Oh come on, he's good for her."

"Meh," Romeo said, with a careless shrug of his shoulders. "He's alright."

"You love him and you know it." Amanda smiled.

"Yeah well, I can't hate him forever. Sarina would never talk to me again."

Amanda rolled her eyes and slid her arm through his. She loved him, even if he was twice as stubborn as any man she'd ever met, human or not. Had it really been nearly twenty-eight years since he'd all but forced her to marry him? Okay, he'd been nearly irresistible, but still; he'd also been an annoyingly arrogant dick. "Would you have picked anyone different?"

He turned those smoky eyes on her and set her insides fluttering with his crooked grin. "Honestly? Never. I wasn't about to tell her that. But Brody fits her to a T and…," he paused with a sigh, "you were right."

"Excuse me?"

"When you said she'd hate us; that we'd destroy any trust she had in us. You were right."

Amanda smiled, but not laughingly. It had certainly been a tense moment in their family.

If only she'd known then how much more tense things would get from that moment on, perhaps she'd have been somewhat prepared. The last three years had been both joyous and torturously painful. She'd welcomed two healthy, bouncing grandsons into their pack, thanks to Sarina and Brody. She'd also buried her eldest son, Sarina's twin, Jason. She'd fallen apart and somehow put herself back together after his death. Now, things started to settle down. That is, until last night when she visited the special room and spoke to the beautiful keeper of that room. Amanda sought her council after suddenly feeling the weight of worry that Sarina was not actually *her* Sarina. The bond between mother and child is one of the strongest and purest in nature, and when she went to hug Sarina earlier that evening, she felt something missing. A feeling of warmth and sincerity that was non-existent.

Faced with terrifying knowledge that Lilith had managed to convince the Devil himself to allow for her to inhabit Sarina's body, and therefore also aiding in the eventual destruction of the entire Traverse family,

Amanda had no time to waste. Torn between saving her daughter or ruining a joyous occasion her family was looking forward to, the latter would have to wait. Of course it could wait! Her daughter was being held captive in purgatory! Giving her head a shake, she wrung her hands as a worried look furrowed her brow. She decided to broach the subject with Romeo with the most delicate touch, so as not to anger him beyond control, especially when he found out that Lilith was behind it all. She couldn't risk Lilith using her incredible power to keep Sarina a prisoner forever, or worse, end her daughter's life altogether. Lilith could be unpredictable and extremely dangerous if she knew Amanda and Romeo were on to her, especially before Amanda was prepared with a plan to save their daughter.

"You're brooding again," Romeo said as he drew her into their room. "Not that I don't find it incredibly sexy."

Amanda giggled when his lips found the nape of her neck and his arms came around her waist.

"Your mind is so sexy when you're brooding. Wanna do some brooding in the buff?" he asked.

"And you're incorrigible. But you did get me to stop brooding, for a minute."

"If the promise of sex keeps you from sulking, I can make good on it," Romeo said teasing, playfully nipping her shoulder.

Amanda sighed, wishing that an afternoon romp would cure all her worries. "I just… ever since we got back from defeating Fenris, I just can't shake the feeling that something's not right. I haven't said anything before now, because I wanted desperately to deny it. Now though, that feeling's getting stronger almost by the minute."

"Have you done any spells to expel it?"

"No," Amanda said, not sure she could explain why. She knew she had to try though, for everyone's sake. "I know this sounds crazy, I've almost convinced myself that it is, except I know in *here* it's not." She placed her hand over her heart.

"Well?" Romeo urged.

"I think there's something wrong with Sarina."

"But you don't know what?"

"Right," Amanda sighed, even though she knew this was not entirely true.

"Maybe we can work together to narrow down what the difference is. I don't suppose we could chalk it up to her excitement about the wedding?"

"No and that's just it. She doesn't seem excited. Two weeks ago she appeared ready to just get on with it. I figured after nearly three years together, maybe it was just a formality to her. But then, as everything settled down she was beaming about it. Now we're back to *'I couldn't give a shit.'*"

Amanda knew pretty much what he was thinking when she looked at Romeo. She didn't need telepathic abilities to know what was on his mind.

"Maybe we've all been a little too relaxed," he finally said, his dark eyes meeting hers.

"You think something's wrong as well." It wasn't a question, but a statement of undeniable fact.

"I think you're not the only one who's noticed changes," he agreed.

"Why didn't you say anything?"

"Because she already thinks I'm paranoid. I wasn't sure what I saw was real or if it was just a figment of my imagination."

"So what do we do?"

"What else? We confront her with something she wouldn't know unless she was our Sarina."

"Such as?"

"What it was like when she was with Brody that first time," Romeo said, refusing to flush at the idea of his daughter being with a man. "Only our Sarina would know the answers to those sorts of questions."

"You want to question whoever is pretending to be our Sarina with intimate questions about her first time. Any woman can answer those questions." Amanda balked at this suggestion.

"Not the way our daughter can," Romeo said, grinning when Amanda sighed.

"Have fun with that one," Amanda said in retort, now sporting her own wide grin.

"Oh no," he started, putting both of his hands out, palms facing her. "I didn't say *I* was going to talk to her, I said *we* should. You know damn well I'm talking about *you*, woman."

<<◇>>

Amanda's laugh poured out so naturally that Sarina felt tears sting her eyes. She might not have had the body she once did, but her emotions were still her own and they were heightened, especially given the circumstances. How do you convince your mother that you were real and not a figment of her imagination when she can't hear you? Brody had believed her, but he'd been able to hear her, even to see her somewhat. Telepathy, through mates, was a natural part of being a werewolf. She just hoped her mother could hear her as well. There was hope, knowing that her mother was a Radiant. It wasn't the first time she'd been able to hear someone she loved, despite great obstacles.

Sarina remembered her mother telling her that when she'd been pregnant with Sarina and Jason, Amanda had been tucked safely inside the in-between realm in Ireland. Even then, she'd been able to step outside that space to hear Romeo. It had held her together over the months of their separation when he'd been held prisoner by her Aunt Aurora's obsessive ex, Remus.

That time seemed like forever ago and Sarina felt her heart drop again when she thought about her now deceased brother. The mere fact that she hadn't seen him in the underworld was cause for celebration, but her heart wasn't in it yet. She needed to get her life back and her mother was her only hope of doing so.

Chapter Two

Amanda stepped out of her room and instantly shivered as a cold, nearly frigid, burst of air touched her skin. Her senses were pricked and she stopped, listening carefully for any sound that seemed out of place.

"Sarina?"

The cold moved from the center of her body and seemed to focus on her cheek, as if someone was touching it.

Mama.

The single word was less than a whisper, so faint that Amanda wasn't sure she hadn't made it up.

"Sarina? Are you okay? What happened to you? Where are you?"

The next words she heard were, *help* and *body*.

Looking up at the ceiling, Amanda knew then that her Sarina was in danger. Whoever or whatever was in her body, it wasn't her daughter. Immediately she got Romeo involved.

"You're saying that Sarina, our Sarina, isn't the young woman who should be sleeping next to her mate upstairs?" asked Romeo.

"I'm saying that our Sarina touched my face with a hand, made of the iciest breeze I've ever felt. She said she needed help and there's something to do with her body. I'm guessing that she's been pulled or kicked out of hers by whoever took up residence in her."

"So how do we get it out and Sarina back in?"

Amanda sighed. She loved Romeo. Never once had he questioned her, or made her feel insecure. He'd loved her well and supported her in every decision, even when he'd disagreed with her method. He'd been the first to trust her abilities and she knew now he trusted her instincts.

"We need to exorcise whatever's holding her body captive," Amanda explained. "It's not going to be easy, because whenever a demon or entity takes over a body, their actual survival depends on locking that person out or away. If someone has managed to kick Sarina's spirit from her body, getting her back in will take everything I have in me."

"Tell me how to help," Romeo replied, his light eyes simmering. Another alpha trait, Amanda now admired. At first, she'd seen only the arrogance and ignorance. He was so full of himself back then that it overflowed until everyone, including her, wanted to punch him in the face.

Now that arrogance paid off in the cocky way he always backed her up. Never, since the day they'd mated had she ever doubted whether or not he would support her. Be it a decision about their children, her powers, or their pack; Amanda knew that she would always have an ally in Romeo. It was just one of the things she cherished in their marriage.

Brody sat up and looked down at the woman sleeping in his bed. On the outside, she was Sarina, his stunning, gorgeous mate. Her long, flowing hair lay over her shoulder and spilled across her pillow. Her lithe body still turned him on, even after carrying and delivering twins. Sighing, he knew it was the woman inside that beauty though, who had truly captivated him and whoever was there now wasn't his mate. He'd have known sooner if he hadn't been so enamored with the idea of finally having peace and quiet.

His whole relationship with Sarina had been so full of drama, battles and stemming all-out war that Brody had wanted desperately to have this time. To nurture what he'd wanted from the beginning, a chance.

She stirred and stretched, a smile forming on her lips. "Good morning handsome," she cooed.

Brody nearly fell for it, until Sarina's face filled his memory. Her words echoed in the back of his mind. He felt like jumping out of the bed as if it was on fire but he didn't want to arouse her suspicions. Instead he stretched and made an excuse about getting a shower.

"I smell," he simply said.

"Want some company?" asked Sarina.

Inwardly he groaned. He wanted Sarina so bad his body ached for her. "Nah, I won't be long enough for that. Some of the pack members need repairs on their homes so I'm gonna grab a quick bite to eat and then I'll be out."

"Alright," she said smiling and gave him a wink. It was so much like what Sarina would do that turning away from her was the hardest thing he'd ever done. He shut the bathroom door and sighed. He had to convince Amanda and Romeo that their daughter needed help. True to his word, he made his shower ten minutes and was downstairs in fifteen. He grabbed an apple and a muffin and started toward the parlor when he spotted Amanda and Romeo heading his way.

"We need to talk," said Brody.

They closed the doors and locked them. Amanda put a spell on the doors to bar their voices from traveling outside the room. "It's about Sarina," everyone said in unison.

"You know?" they asked of each other.

"Sarina came to me this morning as an ice cold wind. She said 'Mama', 'help' and 'body'. I'm guessing, but I think she needs help with her body."

"Sarina is trapped in the underworld," Brody informed them, "by Lilith and whatever devil she's aligned herself with. Whoever he is, he must be pretty damn powerful to pull off a stunt like this. We may need more help than we have at the moment. Apparently, from what Sarina says, Lilith agreed to help him get all of us if he gave her one last chance to prove that she could take down the Traverse line."

"I can deal with Lilith, especially trapped inside Sarina's body. Do you know what she's planning?" asked Amanda.

"I'm not sure," Brody said with a sigh. He paced across the room and turned back toward them. "Whatever it is, it's not good. Not that I'd expect it to be."

"Why can't that bitch just leave well enough alone? How many damn times do we have to kill her for it to stick?" said Amanda.

"I'm not sure," Romeo finally said, "But I'm going to make sure of it this time." Before Brody could stop him, Romeo was through the double doors and up the stairs, nearly knocking Sarina's bedroom door from the hinges when he barreled through it. Already regretting it, Romeo was too late to keep himself from seeing his oldest daughter's naked backside before he closed his eyes. Still, his indignation came through in the command his voice held.

"Hey Dad," Sarina said in a way that made it hard for him to see her as anything but the little girl who'd come so quickly into his life. Focusing his mental clarity, he pressed on.

"Don't you dare call me that," he growled, nearly changing into his wolf as he did so. "I am fairly certain that you aren't my daughter, no matter how much you look like her."

"Okay," she laughed. "Dad, I get that you and Mom have been under some uber stress lately with Fenris and all, but really? I'm just about to walk down the aisle to marry my best friend. Haven't we all been through enough?"

Romeo ignored her state of undress and pinned her against the wall, his massive hand clamping easily around her throat. "You won't be walking anywhere, you harlot," he growled in a low, menacing voice. It happened so fast that if he'd been questioned sometime later about his certainty of the event, he wouldn't have been positive at all, except he'd caught it in that instant. Her eyes had changed and he'd seen Lilith under the mask of his daughter's face. The fierce growl that rent the air was as vicious as Romeo had ever let go, as anger and fear mixed a wicked concoction in his stomach.

Amanda stood back and watched her husband with an admiration that didn't need words to be expressed. Still, she needed to save her daughter's body from being permanently disfigured by her father's anger and there was only one way to ensure that Lilith never, ever had the chance to scratch and claw her way out of the pits of Hell again.

"We need to take her down to the room," she said, absorbing the steely look Romeo threw her way. Years ago she would have cowered under that dangerous stare. Now she stood her ground and waited. Amanda held out a blanket and Romeo unceremoniously pushed the witch into it to conserve what modesty Sarina would have left when everything was done.

"Lead the way," Romeo said, his voice still harsh. Amanda could tell though that the anger was edging itself away. Deep down, Romeo knew that when everything was said and done, his daughter would need her body.

Amanda turned without another word and headed down to the room she'd created just for occasions like this. She'd never expected to need it this way, but then again, she'd never much expected any of this, truth be told. "From here on, it's just the three of us," Amanda said, stopping both Romeo and Brody at the door. I won't come out until Lilith is back in Hell where she belongs and we have our daughter back."

"Make sure of it," Romeo said as he embraced Amanda, pressing a warm kiss against her startled lips. Pulling back, his blue eyes held all he felt for her.

Amanda stepped through the door and didn't have to click the lock to seal the door. It wasn't the first time she'd used the room, nor was it the first time Sarina had stepped foot into this magical place.

Chapter Three

Amanda lifted her arms and power arced out, washing the room in bright white light. Without her fellow Radiants here, it would take every power she had to do what she had to, but this room, this sacred place would help. In the brightness she could see Sarina's body clearly and also the mirage-like outline of Sarina's spirit. The urge to talk to her firstborn was nearly overwhelming, but Amanda knew one slip, one falter and Lilith would be beyond her grasp again.

Chanting under her breath, Amanda felt her powers ebb in waves that turned the room various shades of pink, purple, orange, blue, green, and red. "Ancestors of Fenris and Lilith, hear my cry. Come close to receive this alibi. Shelter Sarina Traverse here, until she remains solid and clear. Right this wrong once and for all, help me send this demon back to Hell. Keep her there for the wrongs she's done and call out any that can be undone."

The wind that rushed through the room swirled and kicked like a tornado as Amanda fought the war of her life to expel Lilith from Sarina's body. One by one, the dead began to show themselves, each one helping Amanda pull Lilith from Sarina's flesh. Amanda smiled when she saw Aunt Mabel. Then Lucia and Brianna's mothers came as well, each lending their aid as best they could. Thousands of spirits appeared, some in groups, to give Lilith her due. It was then that Amanda knew for certain that Lilith would never bother them again after this. Then the crackle of lightning split the air, leaving the smell of ozone lingering as the woman in white, someone Amanda called "friend", stood in their midst.

"We here have heard your cry," the woman said, comforting Amanda as her words soothed away the sadness from Jason's death and her worry over Sarina. "We will stand witness to the crimes this were-vampire has committed and our judgement will be swift and final."

Amanda bowed before the radiant woman and then stood like a prosecutor and delivered Lilith's crimes. Much like a movie reel, they played throughout the room as Lilith was forced to show her true self. It took some time to deliver all of Lilith's crimes to the woman who stood between the here and now and whatever lay beyond this life. Although time all but stood still in this magical realm, Amanda knew this time Lilith wouldn't escape the judgement that was due her.

"Lilith!" the woman said. Her lips never moved, but her voice boomed like thunder. Electricity crackled like tension in the air as Lilith fought to stay as she was, locked tightly inside Sarina's body. "Come forth and free Sarina Traverse from your torment."

Amanda was in awe. Whatever powers she possessed seemed dwarfed by this magnificent woman. Still, she could tell that Lilith had a plan and it wasn't a good one. Her laugh, the pure evil in it made Amanda cringe.

"Do you honestly think you have what it takes to put me down?" asked Lilith. Just then, she released Sarina's body and speared up, her newly acquired wings flowing out like a dragon. "You know nothing of the power that I claim," she said, her tongue flicking out like a serpent. "You and your pesky, insignificant pack will beg for mercy, which I might decide to bestow."

"Match her," the bright woman said to Amanda. Sarina, who was once again inside her body could barely stand, her physical state weakened greatly by her prolonged absence. She watched her mother and Lilith war with each other, almost desperate to lend her aid. She knew the power that spread through her like water, as if it was as much a part of her as her blood and bone. Had she ever thanked her mother for this gift? A small chant had her body invigorated and she stepped over to her mother, meeting her beautiful green eyes with a knowing grin.

Sarina knew whatever powers they had, she and her mother were all the stronger together. Grasping Amanda's hand, Sarina felt power zing down her arm like a bolt of lightning. Rich and heady, she matched her own abilities with her mother's and soon white hot light shot out from both women's palms. Lilith cursed when that light hit her square in the chest. Her wings swept out, moving her from one spot to another. Sarina tracked her well and Amanda followed her lead. Within minutes they had Lilith on the ground, all but begging for her life.

"I don't know how to be anything else," she wailed. "It was all Fenris!"

"Fenris was banished and if he's smart he'll take the out he was given and live his life in relative peace. You will never know the freedom you could have had, had you left well enough alone. You, Lilith Maggie McDera, are yourself banished from this realm. Never again will you set foot in the land of the living, human or werewolf. You will never torture another soul as long as my line lives."

Sarina, her own body tiring, watched as Amanda raised her hands, light exploding from her being. It spread through the room like a wave, blotting out anything and everything until every square inch of space was covered in the purest white light. So intense was it, in fact, that Sarina was forced to close her eyes for a moment. "Lilith Maggie McDera is, from this day forward, dead, deceased, passed on. Her spirit is and shall forever remain in Hell where she was first banished. As long as the Traverse-Duscene line survives, you will never see the light of a day here, nor will any from your original line with Fenris. Evil is stopped here today and with the cleansing of this room, every last vestige of your line will die with you."

As if the light couldn't possibly get brighter, Sarina felt the heat and heard Lilith's scream as a burst of flaming white light consumed the dragon she'd been. In just minutes, Lilith had burned away until nothing, not even ash, was left behind. Her existence, for all it had been, had finally finished.

Sarina, so relieved at that moment, faltered and fell to her knees. Immediately she felt her mother's arms encircle her. "Oh my baby," she cooed. "I'm so thankful you're alright."

"I wouldn't have been if you hadn't listened to your heart."

"You're my heart, you and your siblings, your father. Without all of you I'd have nothing left to live for."

"I know how you feel," Sarina sighed as she rested against her mother. "Jed and Brody Jr. are my lifeline, their father as well."

"Sarina…" Amanda started. Sarina could hear the caution in her voice as she continued. "You realize that Brody didn't know you weren't yourself. You can't blame him for—"

"I know, Mama. We've already talked about it. I didn't expect him to have stayed chaste in our bed when he didn't know the difference. Lilith is… was, a very persuasive seductress."

"Maybe," Amanda said, her voice lethal. "But the love you two share can undo any whore's game. Don't you forget that, darling. It's *you* Brody wants, not just your body."

"I know," she replied.

"I'm going to send Brody in when I leave. Spend the night here… find what she tried to take from you."

"Alright," Sarina said, easily acquiescing. She didn't have it in her to fight, even if she'd wanted to. When Amanda stepped out, Sarina turned to face the woman in white.

"You certainly changed." Sarina didn't have it in her to be nice, to pretend that this woman who'd banished Lilith to Hell wasn't the same woman who'd sent her there.

"My master released me," the glowing figure replied. "I no longer take orders from him. He said I wasn't useful to his plan, so now I'll work to make sure whatever he's planning isn't allowed to take place. As long as I live, none of the Traverse or Duscene line will suffer because of anything he tries to do, at least not while in this room."

"Is this a gateway then?"

"Of sorts," she said with a smile. "There are others, more powerful than here. But this certainly opens itself up to that realm. You can't have magic in your life without accepting the bad things people and demons alike can do with it."

"So you're on our side now?"

"I always was," she replied. "Even before I made you choose the reality you most wanted, I watched over your mother and her aunt before her. I've watched over your grandparents and theirs as well, as far back as the beginning of your line." The woman paused to reflect on her memories.

"Before now, I was always doing so as an informant, for him. Despite keeping my details to a minimum, I couldn't do anything he didn't allow me to. Now, I'm my own person. I will no longer provide him with anything to aid him."

"I'm glad to hear it," Sarina said.

Amanda let Romeo take her hand and lead her to their room. "They get tucked in?"

"I think so," she said, a smile gracing her face. "It'll take a day or two to really believe that Lilith won't come back around just for spite. I'm not sure Sarina realizes yet that this is permanent. I want to make sure she knows, truly in her heart, that Lilith will never, ever touch what's hers again."

"And you're positive, really positive that Lilith can't come back?"

"She'll never step foot or any other appendage, outside the gates of Hell. I'm almost positive her captors won't be in such a forgiving mood this time around. If there really is a pit down there, I'm sure she's roasting in it right now."

"Well isn't that a pretty picture?" Romeo said, feeling satisfaction in his heart. Amanda accepted his kiss and drew him closer. On a sigh of regret, she pressed her forehead to his, "I have to check on the boys. I promised Sarina I would."

"We'll both go. Then I'll talk you out of that pretty outfit."

"This?" Amanda chuckled. "Please. I've had this thing for years."

"And it's beautiful, because a) it still fits you and b) nothing looks bad on my wife."

"Well when you put it that way." She gave a knowing smile.

They tiptoed up to the room that had been guarded by sentries around the clock since Jason's death. Walking quietly into the room, they looked down at two beautiful sleeping little boys who were the perfect mixture of their handsome parents. Brody Jr., who was nearly the spitting image of his father, slept on his side like Sarina, while his twin brother, Jedidiah -his mother's carbon copy - slept on his back like his father, Brody. Together they kept one another company and comfortable in sleep.

"We'll wake them if we stay longer," said Amanda.

"Well in that case, let's vamoose, baby," Romeo said with a grin. He all but chased her from the room and had her giggling by the time they reached the quiet, soundless refuge of their room. "How did we ever manage to make five beautiful children?"

"I did it in three pregnancies," Amanda chuckled. "That's how. Or don't you remember?"

"Hmm," Romeo teasingly growled. "I certainly remember all the fun we had trying."

Amanda chuckled, allowing him to pull her close and remind her just how much fun it had been. By the time morning came, the Traverse home was blessedly quiet and everyone greeted the day with a renewed sense of calm.

"Now this is living," Gina said without a care in the world, her chair positioned close to Turk. He'd agreed to submit to the rule of the Traverse clan and had shown himself to be trustworthy, something that had amazed nearly everyone. Only Gina had seen the goodness in him. Tall, dark and muscular, Turk had proved to be one hell of a helper. He was adept at carpentry and would be able to assist Brody in fixing up any homes that had damage or any new ones that needed to be built.

"I couldn't agree more," Romeo said as he forked scrambled eggs into his mouth. "Sarina and Brody up yet?"

"We're here," Sarina said, kissing her dad on the cheek as she and Brody took their seats. She winked at Gina who blushed. "So cousin, tell me your plans."

"Um," Gina stumbled. Turk came to her rescue, something Sarina greatly approved of.

"I'm going to ask permission to marry her as soon as her parents return. If they take too long, I'll send word and ask you, Mr. Traverse, if that doesn't bother you."

"Gina's my niece, young man," Romeo responded with authority. "Truth be told, I couldn't have picked anyone better for her. You should ask her parents first, but failing that, you absolutely have my permission."

Sarina beamed at Gina's happiness. She knew what it was like to long for love, compassion, sex even. The fact that Gina had found it, and with a werewolf to boot, spoke volumes about the similarities between humans and their werewolf counterparts. Perhaps there could be some intermixing without jeopardizing either species. After all, without humans, werewolves wouldn't have taken so well.

"Thank you, Uncle Romeo," Gina said, tears brimming her eyes.

"You're welcome, my dear."

Chapter Four

Two days flew by and Saturday dawned gorgeously sunny and warm as Sarina sat in a chair, her hair up in huge rollers. Her Aunt Aurora was smudging a smoky eyeshadow over her lids to bring out her light green irises. Her lips had already been stained a red rose hue and the last thing to go on was the necklace her mother would put on just moments before she walked down the aisle.

"You are breathtaking," Amanda said with a sigh, her tears quickly patted away with the tissue in her hand. "And here I told myself I was done crying."

"Me too," Sarina said, giving in to the happy tears that started to well up in her eyes. Her makeup was redone and half an hour later she stood in front of a huge mirror looking at herself in her mother's dress. New pearls had been sewn on so that it looked as if the dress had been dipped in a pool of them. Her hair hung in soft curling waves halfway down her back. Her mother's necklace, one that had been handed down from her grandmother, hung around her neck. It sparkled and twinkled in the sunlight that streamed in through the huge windows in her old room.

The morning after their encounter with Lilith, she and Brody had moved their little family back to their own house. Now her room had become Amanda's studio as she'd taken up painting to kill some of her down time.

"You ready?"

Sarina turned to see her father standing in the doorway and smiled.

"I'm ready." She could barely speak, nervously smoothing down the skirt of her dress. Romeo Traverse, alpha of the Delta pack, looked impeccable in his tailored tux. "You're looking mighty good, Dad."

"Oh sweetheart," Romeo said, his face caught between pride and heartache. "You are breathtaking and thank you for the ego boost."

Sarina felt her heartbeat start to speed up with anticipation as she took her father's arm.

"Think Brody will like it?"

"I think Brody would have to be six feet under for a hundred years in order to not be effected by you, darling."

Sarina beamed at her father's words. Leave it to Dad to cheer up a nervous girl.

"Don't be nervous. In a matter of minutes the formality will be over. Then we can party."

"No one throws a party like us Traverse's."

"Damn right," Romeo agreed.

The ceremony, just as her father had promised, lasted all of ten minutes from the very start, until they walked down the aisle as Mr. and Mrs. Brody Chase Duscene. The boys, dressed in their matching tuxes, danced right along with their adult counterparts and even tried howling as the moon rose high in the sky. Appropriately on a full moon, Brody and Sarina enjoyed their nuptials.

"I have to admit, I'm surprised that you'd pick a full moon for a ceremony so special and long overdue."

Sarina turned to see a gorgeous, older version of her mother standing behind her. "Do I know you?"

"Not well enough," the older woman said, sadness lingering in her eyes. "I died long before you came into the picture. In my own way, however, I've kept an eye on you and your family. I'm your maternal grandmother, darling. Someone who helped pass those lovely powers onto you."

"You were a Radiant," Sarina said with a sigh, reverence thick in her voice. "Thank you."

"Your thanks isn't necessary, but it's appreciated all the same. I want you to know that Lilith was one wickedly evil woman, but she is the least of your worries. Your mother and father have forgotten that they are not human. If anything, tonight should drill that point home when your father and your husband make the change."

"Is there a problem with the humans around here specifically?"

"As they become more mobile," the woman said, "I'm afraid those who see our kind as a threat will either kill us off like a witch hunt, or simply legislate us into extinction. The ones around our region are of the most immediate concern as they are closest to us. However, humans in general, across our great country and out in the rest of the world need to have an eye kept on them to say the least."

"What can I do?"

"Warn them, remind them that there are stark differences between us and that being friends, even friends with that understanding, might prove to be more dangerous than they'd hope."

"Alright," Sarina said, shaking her head in agreement. "I'll tell them." Sarina didn't know exactly what to say or do. Her hands trembled as she stood there talking to her deceased grandmother. "I'm sorry, I just..." Tears choked her words and Sarina gasped when strong arms wrapped around her. Turning, she saw Brody standing behind her, a soft smile tugging his lips.

"You okay?"

Sarina turned back around, but her grandmother was gone and the moment, so precious to her, was over.

"I'm so happy," she said, bringing her mouth to his. "I'm Mrs. Brody Duscene. Nothing is spoiling this night."

"Even though we have to change?"

"I'll be here when you come home. Tonight and every night with a burning candle to welcome you back."

"Does that candle come with a little romance?" Brody asked, making Sarina smile when his eyebrows wagged at her.

"Maybe," she said with a grin. "It'll depend on how I'm feeling and if I'm even awake. I'm beat."

"Even after the other night? I've never felt more rested."

"Yeah well, you're not the one carrying a baby in your belly now are you?"

"A…a baby?" Brody stammered, his hand instantly, protectively settling over Sarina's middle. "You're sure?"

"As sure as I need to be, yes."

"Have you told your parents?"

"No," Sarina said giggling. "I thought this baby's father might want to be the first to know."

Sarina caught the instant the light in Brody's eyes dimmed and her mind knew what he was thinking. Smiling, she rested her hand against his cheek, enjoying the two-day stubble that grew there. "This baby is *our* baby," Sarina assured him. "There is no way that I'd know I was pregnant this quickly if Lilith had mothered this child. And regardless, she's dead and I'm me again and I'm not a firm believer in nature versus nurture."

"You're not?" Brody asked, seeming truly amazed.

"No," Sarina said. "Why would I be? We're werewolves Brody. There's no nurture in that. It's natural to us, like breathing. Humans, they'd never understand that level of natural being."

"Ah, I don't know. The humans I've dealt with were cool. I'm not even sure they can tell when one of us is amongst them. If they can, they don't start any trouble. I think the humans, at least the ones around here, want to live in peace."

"My grandmother seems to think otherwise."

"I didn't think any of your grandparents are alive," Brody said, clearly confused.

"They aren't." Sarina tried to explain. She started to say more when her parents stepped off the patio and came toward them.

"Your boys are missing their parents, and we have to get ready for the change."

"I'll be right there," Brody said, thankful when his new in-laws took the hint and left them alone.

"I don't like leaving you alone," he said, clearly remembering the times before when he had, all the terrible times they'd gone through.

"I'm fine." Sarina comforted him. "I'm staying here with everyone for the night."

"But a bunch of women—"

Sarina punched him hard in the arm, cutting off his argument.

"Point taken."

"We'll be fine," Sarina said, smiling. "Plus, I'll probably be up when you get home, planning Gina's wedding."

"Oh?"

"Her parents gave the okay once Dad talked to them. They seem to think that if my father approves, then the man must be amazing. I'm not sure whether they just don't want to worry about it, or if they're ecstatic to have found someone who wants their daughter."

"Sarina," Brody started when she held up her hand.

"I love Gina," Sarina said. "I will always defend her. But my aunt and uncle are a different story. I love them because they're family. That doesn't necessarily mean that I agree with their parenting style or lack thereof."

"I didn't know you felt quite that strongly about it," Brody quipped lightheartedly, holding out his hand. Sarina could tell by the way he tensed that the change was already starting. Holding it off could be painful and she moved quickly to get inside where Brody would know she was safe and secure. He wouldn't make the change until he knew his wife and sons were settled inside the Traverse home.

She watched from the big bay window as her mate and now husband began to shift. It always started in his eyes first, something she still found incredibly sexy, even to this day. His eyes would go from crystal sky blue to a deep amber brown as his wolf started to take over. The rest of Brody's shift came in sections, spreading over him much like a suit of clothes. His once rounded head became a long muzzle and tapered head with massive ears that gave him excellent hearing. Then his shoulders would shift and hunch down as Brody became the alpha wolf he was meant to be, even if he didn't claim the position as pack leader. They both knew he was Romeo's right-hand man, whether he was in his wolf or not. That was all either of them needed.

Sarina, drawn by the constantly present attraction she'd always had for Brody, opened the door and walked confidently to him. As their sons grew into men, she'd begin making her own change again, accompanying him on his once a month hunt. She couldn't help hoping that the baby she carried now would be a little girl. Already having the boys, it gave her freedom to think about a sweet faced, pink loving little girl. Now, however, she knew her place was at home, with Brody Jr. and Jedidiah. Touching his shoulder, Sarina smiled softly as he sat down, towering over her by a good foot. He bent his head and playfully licked her jaw. "I love you," she whispered, wrapping her arms around him. "I have loved you from that first cocky grin. Come home safe to me."

She looked him deep in the eyes as he turned to step up next to her father, who was a stunning alpha male as well. Rarely growing up had she taken the time to admire the stealthy and peaceful way her father did his duty. Now she smiled knowing the two most important and dear men in her life would die to protect their family.

"Brody?" she called. He turned back and waited. "Bring my dad back home as well, okay?"

He bowed his head slightly in understanding and then shooed her back inside with a swish of his long, furry tail. Once she shut the door she watched with her mother and the other women in her family as Brody, Romeo and the other beta and omega males and accompanying females headed off toward the wooded area.

"They'll be okay, right?" Sarina said, turning toward her mother.

"They're going to be fine," Amanda reassured her. "Let's make sure they have some good food when they return. If they don't catch anything tonight, they'll be in dire need of sustenance by the time the sun comes around again."

"True," Sarina said with a smile. "So did you ever find out what was up with Brandt's cabin?"

"Not yet," Amanda said. "I plan on taking a trip out there with your father this weekend. After tonight though, he might not be up to that long of a journey so soon. The change wears him out in a way it didn't when we were younger. Back then he was almost cocky about it, always swishing his big, furry tail. He liked to think that every female wanted him. Even when he was courting me, he couldn't help but be arrogantly cocky about it."

"Really?" Sarina said, a look of feigned shock crossing her features before she gave a crooked smile. "I'd never suspect Dad of being arrogant and cocky."

"Never." Amanda snorted. Together, with Gina and Shawna, the women made pigs in a blanket, biscuits, homemade sausage, gravy, enough scrambled eggs for an army and chocolate chip cookies.

"So, Gina. Any ideas for your upcoming wedding?" asked Sarina.

"I just can't believe it's only a week away," the pretty young woman said. "Are you sure you don't mind that we're marrying just a week after you?"

Sarina smiled at her cousin. For all the ways she wasn't like them, she was the best of their family where it mattered.

"Absolutely not. By next weekend I'll be an old married woman."

"Please." Gina giggled. Then her cheeks filled with a blush that had Sarina's eyebrow rising. "Turk hasn't touched me. He said we should wait until we're married."

"That's commendable for a man like him. It can't be easy waiting."

"It's not." She blushed again. "But neither is the prospect of being bedded by a man like Turk. I love him, but I'm nervous."

"Every woman's nervous her first time," Sarina tried to assure her. "Unless she's toasted. Even then, the next morning she's probably feeling less than stellar."

"Sarina!" Amanda gasped.

"What? It's true," Sarina said chuckling. "I'm a woman speaking from experience. Brody is… endowed, we'll just say with enough that I was sore the next day, to say the least."

"Please no," Gina blurted with an embarrassed giggle.

"I'm sure Turk will be exactly what you'd like him to be. It's commendable that he's willing to wait until you wed. Mating should be a breeze afterward, considering. So many of us do the mating before the wedding that we don't know what the reverse is like."

"I'll be sure to take notes," Gina said as she carried more trays of cookies to the large dining table that would serve as a buffet for everyone within the next few hours. Sarina chuckled again as she and the women in her family made food for the members of their pack who would be coming back at dawn, tired and hungry. The time they shared was fueled by a mutual love for each other and the Delta pack. They'd added so many new members in just the last year, it was impossible to keep up with the growth, to know every wolf by name. Still, Sarina knew she needed to try. If she and Brody did take over the Delta pack, it'd be imperative to know the members within it.

"How did you do it, Mom?"

"Do what, honey?"

"Learn it all? I can't imagine just stepping into all this as if it was normal. Not when I'd grown up as a human."

"I loved your father," Amanda said, as if that answered all her daughter's questions. "It wasn't easy, nor was it great fun, but it was important."

"Must have been," Sarina whispered. She grabbed a muffin and headed upstairs alone.

By the time Brody shifted back with the rising sun, his whole body felt as if he'd been run over by a steam roller. He ached everywhere, especially his head and he was dog-tired, no pun intended. He wanted a shower, his wife and a bed.

He tiptoed quietly into their room, hoping he wouldn't wake anyone. With their wedding less than twenty-four hours in the past, the Traverse mansion was still packed with family, friends and pack members of the reigning alpha couple. He showered quickly, thankful for the intense heat and high pressured pulse of the showerhead. Romeo Traverse knew how to do up his home to benefit both the human and its wolf counterpart. Brody stepped out, toweled his hair dry and wrapped the towel loosely around his hips.

He turned around and nearly plowed Sarina over in the process. "God, babe!" he yelped. "Are you okay?"

"I'd be better if you came to bed," she said with a giggle. "I haven't been able to sleep since you left."

"Why didn't you join me in the shower then?"

"Honestly?" she smiled. "We've done that a million times. Well, maybe not, but I wanted something different. And I knew you needed the heat to yourself."

"I would have made room for you, love."

"I know," she purred. "Just like I know, without looking, that you're hard as a rock right now. I plan to take full advantage of that fact. Come here, lover boy."

"Gladly," Brody responded, ready to oblige his beautiful mate. Catching her wrist, Brody pulled Sarina closer and captured her laugh against his lips as he drank her in. Her flavor, always that sexy, first slug of it, poured through him like a balm to all the places that hurt. That was just one small benefit of knowing this amazing woman. She could heal him with just the touch of her heart against his. He knew no other woman who could do that. "You taste like blueberries."

"Mom and I made muffins with Gina and Shawna."

"Hmm," he said, smiling and pressing his forehead to hers. "I like muffins."

Her giggle swept over him, pulling out his own smile, despite the bone-tired feel of his body. He kissed her then, needing and wanting that contact in equal portion. He'd spent his wedding night as a wolf. He'd spend the morning after lying in bed with his wife, as long as their sons managed to sleep in. "Think the boys will sleep for a while yet?"

"We can hope," he offered, holding her hand as he led her to their bed. "Think your parents will mind?"

"No one will hear us," she whispered conspiratorially. "Dad had sound-proofing installed after we mated. He said that the last thing he wanted to hear was his children and their mates. It's also the reason my parents' room is all the way downstairs, tucked under the staircase."

"Always did think your dad was a smart man."

She laughed again and Brody drank in the sound. Gone was the shy, insecure girl he'd picked up outside a boutique in town. Now his wife was a beautiful, confident, sexy woman who still turned him on just by being herself. "I'm sure he thinks you're rather intelligent too."

"Uh-huh," Brody smirked, kissing her neck as they walked over to the window. The sun was well up now and time ticked away, but Brody couldn't bring himself to initiate anything more than playful flirtation. Despite their incredible night in the room full of magic, being in reality made him realize just how close he'd come to ruining everything. The thought still haunted him. "You excited about Gina's wedding next weekend?"

"I'll still be flying on the coattails of ours, but yes. I think she's more nervous than anything."

"Weddings aren't too bad. It took us what, three years to get around to ours? She's got nothing to worry about."

Sarina chuckled. "She's not worried about the wedding. She's worried about what happens after everyone leaves."

"Oh," Brody said, desperately searching for a way to change the subject. The more they talked about sex, the more uncomfortable he became. "So, how'd food prep go while I was gone?"

"Oh no you don't," Sarina said, turning around. Her green eyes pinned him to the floor as if his feet were wrapped in cement boots. "You've been avoiding this for days now. Why are you so anxious around me? I know you want me, so what's holding you back?"

Brody sighed. He'd never been good at keeping things from Sarina. Even when Lilith had control of his mind, he still fought for honesty. Secrecy was never a good thing. "I keep thinking about how many times I came close to losing you, especially this last time. What would have happened if you hadn't been able to reach me? What would have happened if Lilith had succeeded?"

Sarina knew intimately the feeling Brody was struggling with. She, herself, had gone through that same line of questioning. On the other side of that internal conversation she'd come out all the more grateful that they'd persevered.

"She didn't," she reassured him, touching his hand. She pulled it up to her lips, pressing a kiss to his fingers. "She didn't succeed and I owe that to you and my mother. Without your intense faith in me, without the love we share, Lilith may very well have pulled it all off. If for only an instant I had doubted what we have, I'd still be in the pits of Hell trying to claw my way out. It's because of you that we're standing here, like this, today."

Sarina watched his blue eyes fill with relief and smiled as tears brimmed in her eyes.

"I've never once doubted anything about you and me," Brody said. "Not even when Fenris and that evil woman turned me into an older man. Even then I managed to catch your interest."

Sarina giggled. "No offense, but I'm thankful that everything went back to normal after that."

"Me too," Brody said with a smile. He pulled her close and Sarina met his kiss with her own need, asking as much as she gave in return. Her arms wrapped around Brody's neck as she opened to invite him deeper. Her lips met his in a heated kiss that teased her senses, bringing to life the hunger that only he could satisfy.

"Make love to me," she whispered against his mouth, loving the spicy scent of his soap. Already her body was primed, ripe for him.

Chapter Five

Brody was powerless against her, had always been helpless to stop the incredible ways she affected him. He let her lead him to their bed where he lifted her up to the mattress so she was sitting, one leg on either side of him. He ran his hands up her thighs, loving the smooth, skin that twitched under his touch. He leaned closer to her, his warm breath touching her skin a moment before his lips. The salty taste of her flesh aroused him as he ran his tongue along the sensitive part of her neck, trailing his way down to her collarbone. Using his hands, Brody tore the seam of her long-sleeved, almost see-through, white shirt, watching as it gave way so he could feast on more of her.

He smiled softly when he felt Sarina start to tremble. After three years together, it still thrilled him that she could want him so deeply. "Do you know how I've wanted you?" he whispered against her ear. Stray strands of her dark hair tickled his lips as his breath caressed her skin. Her soft moan was all the reply he needed as his hands ran gently over his flesh. She stripped him down in ways no one had ever been able to, much more than just the clothes he wore.

Slowly Brody pressed her back into the mattress, enjoying the way her body lengthened for him. Her torso flattened out, showing the light stretchmarks that evidenced the time she'd spent carrying their twins. He kissed her there, playfully licking her flesh. Arousal burst through him when he felt her long fingers slide into his thick hair.

He heard her inside his head, "*Are you going to play all morning, or take what we both know you want?*"

Grinning, Brody looked up into her beautiful dark eyes. Standing again, Brody dragged her body closer, bumping her pelvis roughly against him. "I'm not sure I want to be gentle with you this time, Sarina."

"I don't recall ever asking you to, except that first time."

"Well then." Brody grinned right before he bent forward and grazed his teeth over her ribs. His lips claimed her perky, tight mound and Brody pulled her flesh hard into his mouth. Her gasp only fueled the passion that flamed inside him like fire. It licked at him, taking his need higher in greedy bites. Sarina arched her hips towards him, grinding against his already aching cock. Her own want was as easy to read as his own and Brody reveled in her want. He tortured them both as his greedy hands touched and took her flesh in equal measure.

Running his tongue along the underside of her beautiful breasts, Brody wanted her to never stop moaning in pleasure. Dipping his hand between her thighs, he sank into the flaming heat that told him ever more of her ripe need. Two strokes had her gasping as her hips writhed beneath him. Five strokes had her coming in the palm of his hand.

"Again," Brody growled as he pressed his hard shaft against her thigh. So needy was she that Sarina couldn't even mouth the words that begged him not to stop. He powered through and the words exploded in her head like an atom bomb.

Take me!

Brody readily obliged her. Without waiting, he sheathed himself deep and fast inside the tight walls of her flaming hot pussy. Her upward thrust met him as she took him to the hilt, burying his need fully inside her. Brody used her body, unable to get deeper no matter how he thrust into her. Pulling her hips closer, he sought a union that only Sarina could give. Building her up, over and over again, Brody felt her crest and his own orgasm pushed him over that great fall as he spent himself.

Unable to let her go, Brody trailed feather light kisses over her body and felt his wife clench around his cock, pressing against his sensitive tip. Grinning, he flicked the pad of his thumb over her clit and heard her cuss beneath her breath. Tit for tat had never really been their game, but playing now seemed so right. Still inside her, he bent and took her pouty mouth, sliding his warm tongue easily between her lips.

Her arms came around his shoulders and Brody groaned when her hips slid over his hardening cock. It was quite an experience to feel himself grow hard inside of her, the wet warmth of her inviting body already encasing him.

Sarina knew almost instinctively when Brody would let her lead. He was a `take charge' sort of man, something that was always an attractive quality. But every once in a while he'd give her the reins. It was unspoken between them, but when he let go, it empowered her to be the alpha she was born to be. Considering they both had those qualities in their personalities, it was just as sexy that he could step back and give her the opportunity. When it came to sex, they both won, not that they ever really lost.

Sitting up, Sarina took Brody's hands and placed them on her thighs, enjoying the way they slid along her legs to cup her ass. There really was no substitute for a working man's hands. The men who worked in an office, typing all day, really had no way to compete with a man who used his hands to build and create. She'd take a man with hands covered in callouses over those soft, sissy hands any day. Challenge lit Brody's eyes as she made her needs known and quickly found herself braced between the side wall of their room and Brody's hard, eager body.

Considering she'd never known any other man, even when Brandt had seduced her, she enjoyed the way Brody's body fit hers. Her folds swelled to greet him, already bruised from the pulsating rhythm of their first tussle. Aching, Sarina slid down fully to embrace her mate's hard, throbbing cock. His fullness, shocking during those first few months, now brought Sarina a sense of expectation and she welcomed their lovemaking with the willingness of a happily married woman. Still, the wolf in her wanted something a little rougher than her human was prepared for and without warning her body began to shift.

A howl of pain was all the warning she'd been able to give Brody before her body opened to morph into the animal waiting inside. Normally she shifted her legs and ribcage first, going to all fours as her thick pelt spread across her body. This time though it was her inner organs that changed first and mainly her reproductive organs. They shifted to her spine and lowered to her knees as her legs moved up and back. She felt the baby in her womb move around frantically as her body continued the change. Falling forward she caught herself on her front paws and shook her whole frame as her coat replaced the skin she'd been wearing. Turning, she sat on her haunches, playfully licking Brody from chin to cheek as she whimpered.

"You want to make love like this?" he asked, his face still registering his slight shock. Beautiful eyes stared into her, eyes that never ceased to attract her. Whether wolf or woman, Brody was the only man she'd ever truly wanted. It was not lessened in the least by their extended relationship. She dipped her head once before rolling on her back and showing him her tender belly. For a wolf, the most important sign of submission, male or female, was bearing the underbelly. As the most vulnerable section of the body, exposing the belly to a dominant was a show of immense trust.

Brody's eyes twinkled and then gave his own yelp of pain as his body shifted. Long, muscular legs took on the angle of a dog's hindquarters and a long, bushy tail extended to swish at the air. Sarina watched her mate turn, admiring both his physical strength and the beauty of his wolf emerging. Large hands became huge, man killer paws each sporting razor sharp nails. His chest widened and his ribs thickened to protect all the organs that now shifted down into his belly or up into his chest. When all was done, his vivid blue eyes stared at her from a dark gray coat that covered every inch of him, save the tip of his tail which was a stormy, light blue-gray.

The woman inside the wolf was impressed, as always, with the sheer power of her mate's wolf. He wasn't a braggart and easily stood second in line to Romeo, mainly because he was married to her and she was the next alpha in line. She knew just as well that he would have taken any position in their pack if it meant securing a good leader for his fledgling pack. It was only part of the reason she loved him. He was always thinking of others. It made it so easy to be considerate of him and what she knew he liked. Standing, she brought her wolf to him, touching his nose with hers to signal their relationship and as an offering. As the wolf it was impossible to be together if the female wasn't in heat. Knowing she was brought a sense of excitement to their mating. This time wouldn't last much longer for the animal that nestled inside Sarina. The babe in her womb would signal the end of her heat soon, but tonight she'd give in to the need and enjoy her mate in a way they didn't often indulge in. Knowing Brody was just as into it as she was gave Sarina all the confidence she needed to offer herself this way to him.

Brody's low growl told her he was anxious and needy. She obliged him by circling around him, swishing her tail playfully so he'd catch her scent. As a female, the pungent odor of her willingness was all the encouragement a male wolf needed and Brody was certainly no different. He slapped a massive paw to her hip and pulled her under him, positioning her just right as his other paw secured her other hip in the right place.

Sarina loved this part, that first entrance. Man or wolf, it was never unwelcomed and even now Sarina felt only anticipation. Inside the wolf, Sarina heard Brody's words in her head. "How is it that I can have you and still be left wanting you all over again?" She answered him with a wiggle of her hips and soon the rhythm of their love, the pace of their continuous romance took over as they once again became lovers.

Sarina lay down on her belly after they finished and cherished the afterglow. More than sex, it was this time that she enjoyed the most. Brody, unlike other men she'd heard about, seemed the most talkative now, as if sex relieved all the tension and he could just relax and be, with her. There was no pressure here and Sarina loved it.

Amanda stood on the porch, a light jacket settled over her shoulders.

"You're sure you want to do this?"

She turned at Romeo's voice. "I am. Does that make me crazy?"

"Oh," he chuckled. "Probably not, but just in case, I'll tag along."

"You're damn right you will. Considering I can't see this cabin, I'll need your eyes."

"Well I doubt Brandt and his family would have a problem with you investigating this place. I know they thought of it as home but—"

"True, but still. I need to know that they're okay with my looking into their home, or what passed for it recently."

"Alright then," Romeo agreed. He walked with Amanda up the stairs that led to the suite where Brandt, Carly and their twins were staying. Much like Brody and Sarina's room it contained sound proof walls and a large, private bathroom, convenient for guests on any occasion. Giving a slight knock, Romeo stepped back to wait beside Amanda.

When Brandt poked his head out, he smiled and closed the door behind him as he came out to talk with them. "Hello."

"Hi," Amanda said, monopolizing the conversation. Romeo was more than happy to let her do so, at least she presumed. "I was hoping you wouldn't mind if I, if Romeo and I took a look around your cabin. Before you say anything," Amanda rushed on. "I don't need to go inside. I just, I have some things I'd like to research in and around the area."

"Sure," he said with a smile. "It's not a problem. As it is, it looks like it may be a while before we get back that way anyways. Just let me know if you need to know anything. If I can help, I don't mind."

"Thank you," Amanda said, grinning at his obvious feeling of obligation. She knew it couldn't be easy on him, staying in their home after what he'd done to Sarina. Seduction was one thing. Seducing the alpha's daughter just to try and impregnate her to use the baby as a pawn was something else entirely. "We're grateful." Brandt simply nodded his head before going back to his wife and sons.

"Shall we?" Romeo asked.

She took the hand he offered and together they left the house and started into the forest.

"I don't suppose you could teleport us closer?"

"You don't like walking with me?"

"It's not that, babe."

"Hmm," she replied thoughtfully. "Alright, hold on." Using the powers she was given as a Radiant, Amanda almost instantly transported both herself and Romeo within ten feet of the spot she'd sat with Shawna outside the little cabin in the woods.

"I forget sometimes how that can steal my breath," said Romeo, feeling a wee bit nauseous.

Amanda couldn't help but giggle.

Romeo had always supported her, no matter the issue. But when it came to the powers she wielded like a second skin, he oftentimes had a weak stomach, not that she made a big issue of letting him know she noticed.

"Mine too," she said, softening the blow to his ego. "So, can you see it?"

"I can." Romeo whistled low. "It's a dump, no offense."

"I'm sure Brandt won't mind," Amanda said, reassuring him. "My issue is that I can't see it. I can't even tell that anything is sitting out here in our woods. To me it looks just like every other section. There's not even a smudge or smear to clue me in."

"And this is the same cabin your ancestors talked about in the journals?"

"It has to be," Amanda insisted. "Do you think there's a different one?"

He didn't and that was half the problem. If this was the cabin and he was positive it was, something had to be up for a woman as powerful as his wife to not be able to see it. "I don't think there's a different one," Romeo said with a sigh. "But I'm at a loss as to why you can't see it. Have you asked the other Radiants about it?"

"I haven't mentioned it to anyone, except you. Shawna and Sarina are the only other wolves in our pack who know about the cabin and that I can't see it."

"We need more information about this cabin. Any chance Brandt will talk with you?"

"More than likely," she said, smiling. "I know he's anxious to have his own place. I'm just hoping he'll consider joining our pack and not returning to his dilapidated hunk of junk."

"That makes two of us," Romeo said in agreement. He grabbed Amanda's hand and ushered her along with him. "I'm not sure I want you poking around this place, Amanda."

"Why?"

"Because," he said. "Whatever's keeping you from seeing it, obviously doesn't want someone with power sticking their nose there."

"Maybe," Amanda said, turning to look back toward where the cabin sat. "But I can't rest now, Romeo. That cabin haunts my sleep. Every time I close my eyes, it's there. I'm afraid it'll keep at it until I uncover whatever secrets lie there."

"Maybe, but I'm still not sold on the idea. We'll ask Penelope to take a look and see what's up. If she can see it, but you can't, we'll know it's an issue with just you. If, however, she can't see it, maybe we should leave it alone."

"We'll see," Amanda acquiesced. "But I'm not promising anything."

"I know," Romeo said with a sigh. When they returned to the house, both leaders saw that something was happening. People seemed to be coming from everywhere, piling up around the house like, well, dogs to a new friend.

"Clear the way!" Romeo shouted, holding back a grin when everyone began to do as he asked. Amanda followed him into the house and almost instantly they knew why everyone was heading their way. The sounds of a new baby rang through the air and Romeo could smell the werewolf scent. "I need to see him." As he headed up, he ran into Brody who guarded the door to the birthing suite.

"Sorry, Romeo," he said, a wry grin splitting his lips. "Doctor's orders that no one goes in until the mother is decent and the baby is resting."

"Doctor's orders huh?" he said with a smile. "I'm guessing Sarina has things under control in there?"

"As always," he said with a nod of his head. "It shouldn't be much more than fifteen or twenty minutes more."

"Alright," Romeo said with a sigh. "Y'all know where to find me."

"We do," Brody said, adding another nod of his head.

"Quite sure of yourself aren't you, pup?"

"I am," Brody said, straightening. Normally an alpha who'd given up his rank wouldn't look the King in the eye, but Brody had learned that Romeo wasn't easily threatened by the gesture. "Knowing Sarina, the incredible woman she is, gives me a certain confidence I might not have had before. I owe that to you and Amanda."

"I'm sure she'll be pleased to hear that," Romeo said, inclining his head slightly. "We'll be downstairs waiting."

"Yes, sir."

<<◇>>

Sarina smiled as she handed the tightly swaddled bundle to Brandt. "He's a very handsome boy," she said.

Brandt beamed with pride, taking a moment to look down at the scrunched up face. Sarina knew by the look on his face that whatever had caused him to treat her badly in the past was behind them now. She wasn't sure they'd join her father's pack, but wherever they went from here, they would part as friends.

"Thank you," he said softly. "For everything."

"You're both very welcome," Sarina said, smiling. "Now, you all need some rest, so I'm going to take your two little ones downstairs for some lunch. I'll bring up a tray for you two and some water as well. Brandt, do you want any coffee?"

"God, yes."

Sarina smiled again before leaving the couple to some quiet time.

"How'd everything go?" Brody asked her as she stepped into the hallway.

"Better than I expected, all things considered," she said, smiling as she took his offered arm. "Carly is stronger than she looks. Delivered herself a small, but healthy baby boy. They named him Theo. Theo Jason Medford."

"They knew about Jason?"

"When I was in with Carly, Brandt told me he'd heard the tussle in the woods and had just come out of the cabin to check things out when we were lifting Jason's body up to take him home."

Sarina hadn't expected the wave of grief to crash over her, but it did regardless. When Brody's arm came around her shoulder and pulled her close, she buried her face in his shoulder and wept once again for the brother, the twin, who no longer lived.

"He would have liked this you know… everyone naming babies after him," Brody said lightheartedly.

"Oh, yes," Sarina said in agreement with a teary-eyed smile. "Little bastard would think in his big, airy head that he was more loved than anyone else."

"Probably say something like *it's just because everyone loves me so much*," Brody said with a laugh and trying hard to mimic Jason's voice.

"Exactly," Sarina said, smiling. She reached up to kiss Brody's cheek. "Thank you, for making me laugh and feel better."

"That's what I'm here for."

Sarina grabbed Brandt and Carly's twins on the way to the kitchen and lulled them with promises of warm cookies. They ate the finger sandwiches she made while she ladled two bowls of soup and added sandwiches as well, to a tray she made up for their parents. She didn't often spend too much time thinking about life in the grand scheme of things, but with a new baby in residence, at least for a little while, she smiled at how crazy life was. A man she loathed, a brigand who'd tried to impregnate her, rightfully earning her ire; was now upstairs in her parents' home tending to his wife and new baby. And to cap it all off, they were all, for the most part, friends.

She wouldn't be able to hang out with them in the way she would have with Jason and his mate had he lived, but she knew now that Brandt and Carly would be welcomed with open arms whether or not they decided to join the Delta pack. Brandt was fiercely protective of her and it warmed Sarina's heart to see just how much he'd changed in the two years since he'd talked Fenris into infiltrating her pack to try and impregnate her with a child he would have used as bait.

Chapter Six

Romeo was just wrapping a towel around his waist after a shower when Brody knocked on the door. "Come in," he said, rubbing an additional towel over his shaggy hair.

"I came to tell you, sir, that Carly and the baby are ready for you."

"Excellent," he said, smiling. "Thank you, Brody."

"You're welcome, sir."

Romeo and Amanda knocked gently on the room that had been relegated to Brandt and Carly when they'd come to stay at the Traverse mansion. When they were invited in, Amanda immediately cooed over the new baby, smiling and engaging Carly in conversation about how the delivery had gone and how handsome the little boy was. "May we hold him, Carly?"

"Of course," the small woman said. Having been terribly abused by her original pack for not being able to carry a baby to term, Carly looked resplendent as she handed her son to Amanda.

"I don't mean to rush your decision," Romeo smiled. "But if you're going to join our pack, I need to mark this little guy, sooner rather than later."

"What does that do?"

"It signifies that he is a member of my pack, to be protected and watched over by every member, until he's able to do so for himself. I would also mark your twins. I can assure you it's not painful in the least bit."

Romeo could tell that the new parents struggled with the decision. "I can wait, of course," he offered. "But the sooner it's done, the sooner he'll fall under the protection of our pack. When Sarina's twins were kidnapped, our entire pack slept on the lawn until they were brought home safely. Every wolf has its place, even the smallest of us."

"We've talked extensively about whether our decision to join your pack is right for our family. As you may know, I struggle, especially after Fenris, to align myself with any pack. I have, however, watched your family for a while now and I know that as our family has grown considerably, I can no longer have them live in a damp, musty cabin that's barely inhabitable. Does your pack hunt together or alone?"

"We often hunt in smaller groups. Sometimes couples will hunt together, especially if they're teaching their young during a first change. Sometimes the men will go together or the women who change. This last full moon I hunted with Brody and other members of our pack while Sarina stayed behind with her mother and younger cousin. It just depends. No one, however, is left alone. Safety in numbers isn't just good advice in my pack. We take the safety of our members very, very seriously."

Romeo watched as the couple shared a look that spoke much more than any words. He saw the slightest tilt of Carly's head and held back the grin that wanted to split his face. "I suppose there's more cause for celebration then," Brandt said, smiling. "It looks like you've just gained five new pack members."

"Terrific," Romeo said, cracking a wide grin. "May I?" He reached out toward Amanda and she passed the baby gently into his arms. Then she left the room to allow Romeo to tend to matters. He cooed lightly to little Theo when Carly and Brandt nodded, giving him permission to mark their youngest son. He looked deeply into the child's dark blue eyes, continuing to coo in a chant-like way, entrancing the baby to the sound of his voice. Romeo continued as he breathed in the breath of the small baby and gave back his own breath in return. After a minute or so he looked up and smiled. "It's my great pleasure to say that Theo Jason Medford is now a Delta pack member," Romeo said, handing the small bundle back to his father.

"Can our twins be marked as well?" Carly asked, as she took the fussing baby.

"Absolutely. We can wait until they're just about asleep as it works better that way for older children. Tonight I'll mark them and then tomorrow when you've rested more, we'll do a ceremony for all of you, officially."

"Thank you," Brandt said, a hitch in his voice. Romeo shook his hand, his own emotions swirling.

"I should thank you," he said humbly. "You've honored my son in a beautiful way. Something you didn't have to do."

"Trust me," Brandt said. "It's the least I can do. I owe you more than my meager life is worth."

Romeo rested his free hand over the one Brandt had placed in his. "Then we'll just say that we're both very grateful. Now enjoy your lunch and get some rest. You're going to have your hands full with twins and that little one."

Amanda found Romeo quietly leaving Brandt and Carly's room. She smiled up at him as he descended the stairs. "How are they?"

"Unofficially, they're part of our pack. We'll remedy that tomorrow. For now though, the children, especially little Theo, is a Delta pack wolf. I just marked him as such."

"How terrific."

"You needed to see me?"

"I want to go back to the cabin."

"Already?"

"Yes," Amanda said, steeling herself for what she was about to add. "I want to spend the night there, alone."

"No," Romeo said, not even stopping to debate with her.

"Romeo," Amanda sighed. "I need to see this through. I need to know what this all means."

"No way, Amanda. I worked my ass off to have you, to build our pack, to keep everyone safe. I won't risk my queen, because she has a hunch about a cabin that she can't see."

"Your queen has a name," Amanda said testily.

"Amanda," Romeo said, taking her hands in his. "You know that I want answers for you just as much as you do, but we can't have you gallivanting around the countryside. Not when we're about to induct five new members into our pack tomorrow. You need to be here, to be present."

"And I will be. I'm not talking about moving there. I just need to see what this cabin meant to my ancestors and why I can't see it."

"Absolutely not," Romeo said, his voice telling her his decision was final. A spark of indignation swept through her and he had to grin. No wonder Sarina was the way she was. There was no denying she was Amanda's daughter.

"You know I'll go on my own anyways."

"And you know I'll do everything in my power to stop you," Romeo said, backing her up to the wall near their bedroom.

"Oh?" Amanda tried her best to keep a serious face but a chuckle escaped her. When she found Romeo's eager readiness, a fired mixture of want and need exploded in her inner being. Acquiescing to him and her own fervor, Amanda allowed him to carry her into their room, kicking the door shut with her foot as he did so.

Sarina tiptoed downstairs well after dark for a drink and found her mother rummaging through the fridge in what looked very much like jeans, a t-shirt, a flannel outer garment and hiking boots, if she wasn't mistaken.

"Mama?"

She squelched a giggle when her mother started, hitting her head on the top of the fridge. "What are you doing up?"

"I was thirsty and came down for a drink. What are *you* doing?"

"I'm getting some food."

"In your day clothes? It's nearly two in the morning," Sarina said, nearly cringing at just how much she sounded like the very woman she was interrogating.

"I'm a grown woman, Sarina Mabel," Amanda huffed.

"And yet you still haven't answered my question," she pointedly declared. "You're going to the cabin aren't you? And without Dad." It was a statement, one neither of them wanted to argue about.

"I don't have time to justify my actions to you. Not that I need to, to begin with. Go back to bed, Sarina. Forget you saw me here tonight."

"Nice try," Sarina said with a sly smile. "I'm going with you."

"The hell you are. You have babies who need you."

"My babies are fine with Brody. You're my mother and I'm not letting you go into the woods in the middle of the night to a cabin you can't even see."

"Fine," Amanda bit off. "Hurry up!"

Sarina was downstairs with her own pack in ten minutes, having left a note for Brody and Romeo to follow in the morning. She didn't know why and she knew her mother might hate her for it, but she had a nasty feeling about this cabin when it came to her mother.

"Aunt Pen?" Sarina said when she saw her aunt headed toward them.

"I've been expecting your mother's call for nearly a week now," she said, a conspiratorial smile on her face.

"And Uncle Elijah is just cheering you on from the side lines?"

"Hell no," Penelope Traverse smiled. "I'm sure he'll be hunting me down when the sun comes up, just like your father and mate, if I'm not mistaken."

"True," Sarina said with a shrug of her shoulders. "Alright, we're burning darkness. Let's go see what this cabin has to say for itself."

"That's my girl," Amanda piped up, wrapping an arm lightly around Sarina's shoulder.

Two hours later, Sarina was standing with her mother and aunt outside the cabin that Brandt, Carly and their twins had occupied less than three weeks prior. "I still can't believe they lived here."

"Tell me about it," Penelope said, shuddering. "So, how do we want to do this?"

"Well, I can't see it," Amanda started. "So I need you and Sarina to give me every detail you can about it."

"It's a dilapidated pile of shit," Sarina said with a chuckle, only half kidding. "Seriously Mama, you wouldn't worry so much if you could see it."

"Be that as it may," Amanda said, "I can't see it and for some reason my ancestor's saw the need to keep a record of it. I need to know why."

"So what do you need other than details?" asked Penelope.

"I'm not sure yet, but I figured if you could see it, then there must be some reason I can't. You are my proof checker."

"Great," Penelope scoffed, acting hurt. "Alright queenie, it's only because I love you that I'm doing this."

"And know that I will always appreciate you for it," Amanda replied in return.

Penelope lifted her hands as the wind began to swirl around them. Sarina smiled as she felt her own power begin to sizzle down her arms. Joining her power with that of her aunt wasn't something she was used to, but she couldn't deny how right it felt. Grabbing Penelope's hand, Sarina absorbed the electric shock that zinged up her arm. Instantly, snapshot pictures of the cabin flashed through her mind. One showed a young mother tending to a toddler, her belly swollen with another pregnancy. Her dress was threadbare and her skin was bronzed from spending her days in the sun.

The next picture was of a tall man dressed in coveralls, a straw hat crumpled in his hand. He stood over two graves and hate brewed in his heart. The next picture that flashed showed a massive wolf stalking the cabin. Sarina knew instinctively that it was a werewolf. Just his size was enough to attest to that fact. His dark eyes sent a shiver through her and then, like a movie reel, Sarina watched as he attacked the woman and her small daughter. The woman died protecting her child.

Releasing Penelope's hand, Sarina dropped to her knees and retched on the ground, her body trembling. It took her nearly fifteen minutes before she could tell her mother what she'd seen. Even then tears poured down her cheeks. "The husband had such hatred in his soul. Not that I can blame him really. He came home to find his whole family torn to shreds. It doesn't explain though, why you can't see this cabin."

"We need to try again," Amanda said. "But not now. You two need to rest and recharge. We'll see if we can't do this again in a few days. I need to talk to Romeo and get Brody and Elijah out here as well. All three couples need to understand what this might mean for me and for our pack."

"Where the hell have you been?" Romeo asked, his rage easy to read, even without Elijah and Brody following behind him. "I woke up to Brody telling me our daughter left him a note. And don't you dare take this out on her. She knew you'd need us," he added when Amanda looked sharply at Sarina, who, to her credit, didn't flinch.

"I told you I'd come out here on my own time," Amanda said defiantly. In their nearly three decades together, she'd done little to defy him, especially after they were married. But this was something she couldn't put off or ignore as if it didn't mean anything. "I'm sorry if keeping this from you was my only course of action, but I did warn you in all fairness."

Amanda watched her husband sigh as her daughter and sister-in-law moved to stand by their respective mates. "I'd like to throttle you for scaring ten years off my life, but I'll settle for hearing what you three found out."

"Well," Amanda started, turning for home and waiting for Romeo to join her. She took comfort in him when his hand reached for hers. "We'll have to wait for Sarina to tell that part as it was she and Penelope who were able to see the most. It's still hidden to me, along with whatever happened there."

<<<>>>

Sarina told her father, uncle, and mate everything she'd seen and how she and Penelope had been able to convince the cabin to give up its secrets. "Aunt Pen's got one hell of a grasp on that wind power."

"It only took me the better part of my life to get there, darling," Penelope said with a wink.

"Regardless, you were magnificent."

"Thank you," she said, stopping at the edge of the yard that belonged to the Traverse mansion. "Just let me know when you're up for it again. I'm going home so my man can make me breakfast."

"Uh-huh," Elijah replied with a smile. "We'll see you all later."

Everyone said their goodbyes to Elijah and Penelope as they turned to head into the house.

"We're going to grab the boys and head home," said Sarina.

"You're sure?" Amanda asked, unable to keep her disappointment from showing.

"Yeah," Sarina added. "You have a house full and there's really no need for us to be here anymore, at least not for more than a visit."

"You're always welcome," Romeo said, pressing a hand gently to the small of Amanda's back. "Regardless of the reason."

"Thanks, Daddy," Sarina said, kissing his cheek. "I just think we're ready to be back to our own routine."

"We can understand that," Romeo acknowledged.

It took Brody and Sarina two hours to get the boys and all their belongings collected and say their goodbyes to everyone. Sarina checked in on Brandt, Carly and their children, taking a moment to snuggle the baby.

"You'll be here for the ceremony won't you?" asked Brandt.

"Of course we will," Sarina promised. "How could I miss inducting my favorite new pack members into our family?"

"Your father won't make a big deal out of it, will he?"

"I honestly wouldn't know as I've never seen it done before. When Brody brought his pack here, I spent so much time on making sure they were fed and comfortable that I sort of glossed over all of that. In all fairness there was a whole lot of other stuff going on then, but I can't imagine my dad dragging your induction out or anything. It should be fairly straight forward. Then we can eat."

"Food sounds so good," Carly chuckled. "I have a confession to make."

"Uh-oh," Sarina said, smiling. She sat next to Carly on the bed, admiring the way she took her role for the newborn. "I promise not to hold whatever it is, against you."

"I felt intimidated by you," Carly blurted as if she simply couldn't hold it in anymore. "When Brandt first told me about you, about what he'd done to you; I couldn't imagine a woman who'd let a man do that. Not that I had much room to talk in my condition and circumstances. But I was blown away by your kindness and the ease with which you welcomed us. Even after the twins I couldn't get over how wonderful you were. I just kept waiting for the hammer to drop. I'm thankful that you are as wonderful and amazing as you've always been and that I don't have to worry about some veil lifting to reveal the real you. I'm very grateful to call you my friend."

Sarina didn't know what to say to the fragile woman who was so open with her. Tears stung her eyes as she sat there in the silence. "Thank you," she whispered. "I'm not sure anyone's ever said anything that eloquent about me before. I'm not sure I deserve the praise, but my ego appreciates it." Sarina chuckled as she handed Carly a glass of water. "I can tell you,

Carly, that I am no one special. I happen to be a woman who is also a werewolf and a witch. My mother hasn't really explored all my powers yet, but I'm pretty sure that's all part of my witch heritage. I will tell you though that I want what every woman wants. I want my family to be safe and happy. I want to watch my children grow up and enjoy their lives. And I want to spend as much time with my friends and family as possible. If I can do that, I'm living the dream. I'm thankful that fate or karma or whatever you want to call it, brought us together as I consider you a very dear friend. That being said, get some rest and feed that little guy. I'll watch him for you in a bit so you can get a shower before the ceremony."

Sarina held little Theo as she walked downstairs. When Brandt headed her way she smiled and handed the little boy to his father. "How's Carly?"

"Probably feeling like a million bucks about now. I left with Theo so she could take a shower. She'll be down shortly and then we can welcome you all into the Delta pack in style."

"Terrific."

The ceremony was low-key, much as Sarina had expected. Standing in the back yard with her immediate family and the entire Delta pack spread out all around, Sarina realized how special she truly was. She belonged to the largest werewolf pack she knew of and thanks to her amazing father, things would continue to go on for generations to come. She was privileged to be a part of it, alpha's daughter or not.

After everyone had eaten and enjoyed greeting the newest pack members, along with celebrating over the brand new baby, Brody and Sarina took the short walk back to their own house, their little boys in tow. By the time they got in the door, both boys were sleeping, one in the arms of each of their parents. "How about we lay these two down in our bed and go out back?"

Sarina smiled, knowing full well what her husband had in mind. "I'm game if you are," she replied.

"I'm glad you left the note for me," Brody said, looking her in the eye. "I thought your mom was going to jump out of her skin."

"Me too," she said, laughing. "I wasn't sure how Mom was going to take it, finding out I'd sort of snitched on her. I just couldn't head out there and do what she wanted to do, without knowing there'd be some backup coming, just in case. And I can just imagine how the next little while is going to go. If I hadn't already had the twins, I'd be worried."

"I'm not blaming you," Brody said, touching her hand. "I absolutely agreed that you did the right thing letting us know that y'all had headed out there. If anything had happened, I wouldn't have been able to live with myself."

"Good," Sarina said with a sigh. She stepped up into their hot tub, still dressed in the same dress she'd worn into the woods that morning. "And you already can't live with yourself, well, not productively anyway."

"You don't want to take that off first?"

"Mm-hmm," she cooed. Brody smiled as he headed up to join her.

Chapter Seven

Amanda headed to bed early, claiming a headache from all the activity in the morning. She showered and slipped into her favorite nightgown, burying herself beneath the thick covers to ward off a chill that had seeped into her bones, despite the steamy July temperatures. Sleep swept over her like an evening wrap on a cold night.

She dreamt and saw the visions her daughter spoke of at the cabin. A huge werewolf who tore apart a mother and child, leaving their bodies behind for a broken man to find. But unlike the visions that had stopped then, her dream continued. A man, shattered by the loss of his family, became a hunter, learning and studying his prey like a scholar does his textbooks. He learned of the full moon ritual that brought out the sort of wolves that killed his family and one by one, he took them down. He hadn't the need to hunt like this before and he obtained a silver bullet shooting sniper rifle just for this purpose. As it turned out though, the man was savvy and smart, picking off his prey like deer, one by one.

Amanda shot up in her bed, shaking from the dredges of the dream that wouldn't leave her. She showered, if only to be warm again, and then headed to the kitchen to make coffee and prepare.

"You're up early," Romeo said. A moment later he added, "What's wrong, Amanda?"

"I had a dream that I can't forget and I'm worried that it means more than I want it to."

"Care to share?"

Amanda sat next to her husband, thankful for the bond they shared, even from that first day. "I saw the visions Sarina told us about, but it went further than that. I saw the man, the husband, shooting us, hunting our kind like deer. He had some special rifle that shot huge silver bullets that dropped the wolves he shot with one bullet. I think whoever he was, he passed that hate for our kind onto his offspring. I don't have proof, Romeo, but I feel something terrible coming."

"Well," he said, placing his hand over hers in a show of support. "Then I suppose we need to visit the cabin again and see what else we can learn."

They made preparations that morning and at noon, Amanda, Romeo, Sarina, Brody, Elijah and Penelope all headed out to see about the cabin.

"You think the boys will be okay?" asked Sarina.

"They'll be fine," Amanda reassured her daughter. She couldn't blame her. After the time she'd had bringing them into the world and then having them kidnapped, any mother would be overly protective. The mere fact that she could leave them behind to venture out like this was a testament to her love of family, all family. "Shawna knows who to call if she needs anything and we won't be gone more than a night and a day."

"Alright," Sarina said with a sigh. "Then let's get on with it."

Arriving at the cabin, Romeo, Brody and Elijah worked to set up camp while Sarina and Penelope began the necessary steps to call forth the cabin's memories. It took nearly two hours for everyone to be ready and the men sat back, ready to see what all the fuss was about this cabin. When Amanda stepped in front of them, they cheered, making her laugh at their silliness.

"Gentlemen," she said. "I present the Cabin in the Woods: A Reenactment."

Everyone chuckled and then everything changed as Sarina and Penelope began to chant. The wind began to swirl and sway through the massive trees as Penelope's powers took center stage. Then, like a movie reel, a man appeared before them. The hurt in his heart was so evident on his face that Amanda sucked in a breath.

"It's the man from my dream," she whispered to Romeo.

The man, anger and grief a powerful mixture in his soul, pointed a rifle at a now naked man and growled, "You'll never touch another human soul."

The resounding echo of a bullet leaving the chamber of that rifle echoed in her ears as Amanda watched the werewolf expire. That's how the movie reel played time and time again. Wolf after wolf saw their end the same way, at the end of a rifle that pierced them with such a large volume of silver that they couldn't recover.

When the visions ended and Sarina and Penelope finished, they cleansed the area and came to sit by the fire. "That's what you saw in your dream?"

"Yes," Amanda replied. Continuing she added, "I don't know if the man ever had children, but whatever is coming, there's something brewing between our kind and the human world we live in. I'm not sure we can stem the tide."

"I'm not sure of much," Elijah said, grabbing his wife's hand. "But I'll do whatever it takes to protect Penelope and Jeremiah."

"The feeling's mutual, little brother," Romeo said, giving a shake of his head. "As alpha, however, I have an entire pack to think about. What's best for us, especially if there are people out there trying to pick us off?"

"Should we move?"

"And uproot our entire pack?" Romeo asked. "I'd like that to be the last resort, outside of war, of course. We're tired of war and Fenris and Lilith never actually got that far."

"I can agree to that," Amanda said. "Even without all-out war, we lost good members in just the one major attack. I don't think our pack would do well with another attack like that, especially if the aggressors are carrying silver bullets in their guns."

"We need to learn more," Brody finally said. He'd kept silent for a while, letting everyone else hash it out, but the truth was that his family was just as involved as everyone else. He'd die to protect them and the legacy they were making. "We need some recon."

"Recon?" Sarina asked.

"Some inside intelligence," Brody explained. "We need to send one of us into the human realm to see what's really happening. If a war is brewing, one of us should be able to figure out who's behind it all."

"What about the change that comes over us? We can't have that happening. And whoever we send may need considerable time to flesh this all out."

"I'd like to volunteer," Brody said, not meeting Sarina's eyes. He didn't need to look at her to know she was shocked, as well as, pissed off. "Is there a way to keep me from changing when the full moon occurs?"

"I can check," Amanda said. "But I'm not sure you're the best candidate."

"Why?"

"Because my daughter might skin me alive for sending you into a viper's nest unarmed."

"Who said anything about being unarmed?" Brody gave a sly smile. "As for the rest of it, that's between Sarina and me, no offense."

"None taken," Amanda replied with a light chuckle. Brody had the keen understanding that she already knew the fight that was coming his way and that some secret part of her was rooting for him to win out against it.

<<◇>>

"Are you out of your mind?" asked Sarina.

Brody waited, slowly hanging up his jacket and rolling the sleeves up on his shirt. When he turned around he couldn't keep the grin off his face. "I ever tell you how sexy you are when you're mad?"

"Don't you dare start in on me Brody Duscene! You know damn well that there's no way in hell I'm letting you leave our family for God knows how long. I won't lose you to those monsters."

"Who's saying anything about losing me?" he asked, coming closer to her. She was outrageously sexy, mad or not. "I'm just going to see what they're talking about, listen to their stories, gain some inside information. I'm not going to turn tail and run away when things go bad, if they're even heading there. Just because that cabin keeps showing us a man who was righteously pissed off, doesn't mean that the human race is heading our way with pitchforks."

"And if they are?" she asked, fear coating her skin like a fine perfume.

"Then we'll meet them and hopefully before any blood is shed, we can show them that not all werewolves are evil."

"Our kind has preyed on them," Sarina said.

"Yes, I've been guilty of that myself," Brody said, "until I met you."

"Really?"

"Yes," Brody replied with a knowing grin. "Your pack doesn't feed on humans. I made sure my pack understood that before we joined your pack."

"I didn't know that," she said, stunned. "I just assumed—"

"Right," he said, grabbing her hand. He ran his thumb over the back of her hand, loving the way her fingers flexed at his touch. "Well, your parents helped with teaching my pack members to feed on mainly pigs and cows, and wild game but anything animal will do."

"Huh," Sarina said. "I never really thought much about it before now. To be honest, I never thought much about the co-existence between our two kinds, until my mom went to the cabin. Eating them does make it hard to live and work near them."

"Think that's why no one besides the Delta pack really lives around here?"

"Well, we are a noisy bunch of bastards when the moon's full."

"True that," Brody replied. "So, does that mean we're agreed that I can go get some info?"

"Fine," Sarina said. "But don't expect me to be thrilled about it."

"I won't," he said, his light eyes sobering.

"How do we keep you safe during the full moon?"

"Your mom said that it might be possible to turn off or neutralize my werewolf genes so that when the full moon comes, I won't change. But we'll need to test it this month before I go. Can't risk having me change while I'm in the human world."

"Um, no. That would definitely be bad."

"Yes it would."

The full moon came in July and Brody stayed back with the women, testing Amanda's theory that his genes could be turned off or altered somehow. The moon rose high and beautiful as cool light shone bright in the sky. It filtered in through the double doors and into the kitchen of the Traverse mansion as everyone waited to see if Brody's body would give in to the change or if he'd remain in his human form.

Ten minutes after the moon finished rising, Brody still remained in the flesh of a man.

"Guess it worked," he said. "It's wicked though, on the inside. I can all but feel my wolf stalking around inside. He's none too happy to be cooped up."

"I bet," Amanda said, coming to join him and Sarina in the kitchen. "Still, it's an important step to take. We certainly can't have you turning into your wolf in the middle of what could turn out to be a quiet lynch mob."

"True," Brody said. He looked at Sarina, whose eyes said what her voice wouldn't. He tucked her close and pressed a kiss to her brow. "I'll be fine, sweetheart."

"You're not the one who has to stay behind and wait," she said.

Two weeks later, Brody knew the time had come. The following morning he'd be leaving to hitchhike his way to what was generally referred to as human-country. It wasn't more than fifty miles outside the Delta area, but that fifty mile expanse might as well have been the Atlantic Ocean to most of the wolves that lived inside the New Delta area.

"I still don't like it," Sarina said, her pouty mouth making Brody want to smile. Hiding his grin was a chore when it came to his gorgeous wife.

"I know," he said, moving his hands up and down her arms while they watched the waning moon as it shrank in on itself. "I also know I wouldn't have volunteered if I didn't honestly think it needed to be addressed." Raising her chin with his finger he looked into Sarina's dark eyes. "I don't want to leave with this between us."

She sighed and went into his arms easily. Even hating the idea, Sarina knew she'd never send her man away with angst between them. Still, it wasn't easy knowing how she'd suffer while he was gone. Since the day they'd become mates, the only times they'd been apart had been against her will. She'd never chosen to spend that time apart and even now, it wasn't a choice she'd make on her own. But her pack needed to know what the humans were planning if anything. She wouldn't trust anyone else to get the job done and stay alive doing it. "Promise you'll come home safe to me and I'll put it away."

"Considering you're the only woman I want, the only one I'll ever want, I'd say that's a promise I can commit to."

Sarina felt her heart lurch and then she sighed as Brody took her mouth. The tenderness that oozed out of him wrapped around her like a blanket, comforting her as she prepared to make the biggest sacrifice of her life. She wanted to pull him close and beg him not to go, but that wasn't what he needed to face this. He needed her strength and unwavering support. And tonight he needed the heat and fire they made between them.

Pulling back, Sarina lifted her shirt over her head, showcasing her beautiful breasts and offering herself to him. A grateful smile split his lips, bringing out the small dimple she so loved. Then that fire lit his eyes and his teeth were grazing over her flesh. Ripe for his touch, Sarina moaned when those teeth caught her nipple between them, nipping her skin in all of her most erogenous places. Brody's hands mastered her body as he carried her to their bedroom.

"I'll never have enough of you." It was something Brody said often, but Sarina never got tired of hearing it. She felt the same way, for whenever Brody touched her, she felt like the most beautiful creature on Earth. And now, she knew it didn't matter if she was in her wolf or not, that knowledge remained. Her body hummed as Brody found her most sensitive areas. Wound tight by the way his hands touched her, Sarina exploded when Brody's fingers found her hot and ripe.

"Again," he breathed and Sarina rushed to meet him, her hips bucking hard and fast against him. He wrecked her again, only then demanding the fulfillment of his own needs. Readily she worked to arouse him. Straddling Brody so that her hips sat over his, Sarina slid her wet folds over his length, grinning when he moaned. Over and over again she tortured him, taking just his tip into her entrance before pulling away. Even when he was left breathless, she didn't give him respite. She'd always loved teasing him, but this time, when there was no given length of time before she'd see him again; she wanted it to last forever.

Brody couldn't see straight, such was the torture that his wife inflicted on him. His tip was throbbing as his cock begged to fill her. Fresh off two orgasms, the woman meant to drive him mad with her hot, wet slit.

She just kept rubbing herself against him, as if she didn't know how the whole situation was supposed to go. Surely he wasn't that bad of a teacher. Still, she wasn't letting up and if he didn't change this particular game, he'd come all over himself.

Gripping her lovely hips, Brody picked her up, loving the way she giggled. That giggle strangled on a cry of ecstasy when he brought her wet pussy down on him, impaling her with every inch of his rock hard dick. Again and again he lifted her, enjoying the way her breasts hung in his face as she held onto him. Her beautiful ass smacked against his thighs as she rode him. Already blinded by need, Brody saw nothing but black as he thrust into her at the end, ruthless in his pursuit of their mutual satisfaction. Her cry of his name would echo long after tonight. It would carry him through this next chapter until he could come home to her again.

Morning dawned like any other day as Brody showered. He dressed in jeans, a worn t-shirt, and a baseball cap that covered his blonde hair. "You look so damn normal," Sarina chuckled. "Definitely not like my Brody."

"Daddy," little Jedidiah said, holding out his hands. Brody took him from Sarina and nuzzled his neck.

"You be good for Mommy and keep little Brody out of trouble okay?"

"O-tay," the little boy said. With blonde hair and blue eyes, he was the spitting image of his father and Brody couldn't have been happier about his two little boys.

"Daddy!" Brody Jr. said as he ran toward his father. Brody scooped him up and tossed him in the air. He was dark haired and dark eyed like Sarina, but his spirit was all Brody. "Come back soon."

"I will, buddy."

"I wuv you," he said, piercing his heart, again.

"I love you too and Mommy and Jedidiah."

"Come home soon," Sarina said before she drew him close and kissed him deeply. She clung to him, as if her life were infinitely tied to his. In a way he supposed it was. Without her, he'd be… he'd be dead. Wrapping an arm around her, he pulled her impossibly closer, tasting her with the warm tip of his tongue. When she grazed his lip with her teeth, Brody pulled back.

"I'll only be gone as long as I need to, to get the information your father needs," Brody said, his voice harsh as his emotions began to show. "Then I'll be home to you."

"Good," she said with a smile.

Chapter Eight

Romeo dropped Brody off closer to the town outside their community than anyone inside the Delta pack ever went.

"Amanda said she packed five vials in your luggage and while you only need one, she was afraid it would break. So she sent some backups."

"Awesome," Brody replied through a big smile, hopping out of the truck. Before he could start walking, Romeo stopped him.

"Do what you need to do and then get home, you hear?"

"I do," he said.

"Good," Romeo said, shaking his head. "Then get on with it."

"See you soon," Brody said. He gave Romeo a salute and a wink before he turned and headed to the main road that would take him deeper into town. Brody had the distinct feeling that he was walking toward something much bigger than he'd first thought, but either way, he was about to make history. Either the humans were preparing for war, or a haunted man's wish had died with him and his direct offspring. Brody couldn't help hoping for the latter. Sarina had seen enough war and all of the Delta pack had certainly had their fill of it. Whatever Brody did during this time, he wouldn't take more war back to his people.

<<◇>>

Brody noticed a fragrant odor that got stronger as he got closer toward the town. It was a bright sunny day, but he had walked all morning and was starting to wonder why he didn't have Romeo drop him off closer. Just then, a red, extended cab Chevy Silverado passed by headed toward town. It pulled over just ahead of Brody.

"Use a ride?"

Brody approached the truck. The gentleman in the driver's seat seemed genuine and happy to help.

"I sure could," Brody said, stowing his bag behind the seat. Even with the vials snuggly packed between his clothes, he still couldn't risk them in the bed of the truck.

"You look like you've been walking a while."

"A fair bit," Brody said with a friendly smile. "Started out this morning early. I thought I'd have made it to town by now, but it took me a little longer than I expected."

"Well I'm glad to help," the older man said, holding out his hand. "Kale Pearson."

"Nice to meet you," Brody replied, giving the man's hand a strong shake. "Brody Duscene."

"Nice to feel a good handshake again," the man said with a chuckle. "Not too often that happens anymore."

"My father taught me that you could tell a lot by the way a man, or woman, shook your hand."

"He'd be right about that. Nowadays it's not often I can tell much about anyone anymore. There's some weird shit going on in the world."

"Ain't that the truth," Brody said with a chuckle, finding he liked this man, human or not, just fine. "Just out of curiosity, what is that fragrant smell in the air?

"Oh, you must be referring to the distillery. I've lived here so many years, I don't notice it anymore. It's the town's major industry. The finest whiskey in the region," said Kale.

Brody rode with Kale Pearson into town and checked into *La Blue*. The brochure online had said it was a modest bed and breakfast, a meal Brody hated to miss, and was perfect for the weary traveler. Stowing away his clothes and the vials, Brody headed for the local bar, hoping he'd be able to pick up any undertones about whether the humans closest to his pack were planning an all-out war, or the rumors had died with the man from the visions of the cabin.

"You look like you could use a drink."

Brody turned to see a pretty little blonde take the barstool next to him. Thinking to himself, Brody was thankful to the gods of creation that he was mated to Sarina. His appetite for anyone else was dampened by Sarina's blood that now flowed through his veins.

"I wouldn't say no." He played it light, already knowing what the girl wanted. She barely looked old enough to drive, let alone buy alcohol in a bar.

"Two whiskies, please," the girl said, holding up her hand.

Brody accepted his drink and took in the finer details of the woman next to him. She was small, no more than five feet with blonde hair that wasn't natural. He'd never understood why women always wanted to change things about themselves. The first thing that had attracted him to Sarina, once he got past the scent of her in heat, was her confidence. She knew what she wanted and damn anyone who tried to stand in her way.

"You got a name, sugar?"

"No, sugar isn't my name," Brody said with a smile. "I'm Brody Duscene. Nice to meet you."

"Camille," the girl replied. "Camille Anderson. My daddy runs the town… well sort of. He's the mayor."

Brody downed his drink and was pleasantly surprised. "Damn, that's the best whiskey I've ever had."

Camille smiled. "Would you believe that's our own home town recipe?"

"You're kidding me. This is from the distillery?" asked Brody.

"Yep, you just discovered this town's best kept secret," said Camille proudly.

"So what else do people do for fun here, Camille?"

"Well there's always pool," she suggested. "But if you want some real fun, meet me here tomorrow night at eight." Brody let her write an address on his hand and then watched as she bent over his palm to blow the ink dry. Brody could imagine the young woman getting plenty of catcalls if her mode of dress told him anything. It made him thankful all over again that his first two children were boys. If the baby Sarina carried now was a girl, Brody would have to learn to let go, in a totally new way.

Twenty minutes later, Brody headed back to his room at the bed and breakfast to write down the address and mark a time for tomorrow night. He needed to find out fast whether or not these people meant any harm to his pack.

≪◇≫

"You made it!"

Brody saw the blonde headed toward him and smiled.

"I couldn't miss the real fun," he said, letting her take his hand and drag him through what looked to be a sea of people. His ears, much more attuned to conversation than a human's, picked up several different snippets of information, nothing though that led him to believe a war was coming. "So, Camille. Do you have a boyfriend?"

"Why? You interested in the position?" she teased.

Brody was liking her sense of humor. He was beginning to realize that while he may change into a huge, hairy dog during every full moon, humans weren't nearly as bad as they seemed from a distance.

"I just want to make sure I'm not going to get pummeled for talking to you."

"Mike," she said, looking over Brody's shoulder. Brody turned around and stopped short, noting a mammoth of a man behind him. He came around and stood beside Camille. Easily as tall as Brody himself, the man Camille had called Mike, was built like a refrigerator; wide and all muscle. "This is Brody Duscene. World traveler, come to check out our small corner of the map."

"Hey, Brody," the guy said, nearly shaking Brody's arm off. "Nice to meet you."

"Feeling's mutual," Brody said with a smile. "Camille tells me that this is where the real fun is."

"She'd be right about that." Mike smiled back. "We might be small town folk, but party is our middle name. So, I'm not sure what your preferred poison is, but you're welcome to take your pick."

Brody turned and saw a table with a huge assortment of ales, lagers, liqueurs, wine and hard liquor, just waiting to be taken advantage of.

"Well." Brody tried to laugh. "Y'all certainly know where to make your score. Where the hell all this come from?"

"Everything you see on the table is made here and the surrounding area. Something to do with the water that gives it that special taste. It's getting wide distribution that's the problem. Rumors have been flying around town since forever that there's a pack of real life werewolves just outside of town. No one wants to chance running into one so we never go west of here. Everything we make flows east, which you can imagine, closes us off to a huge market."

"Um, yeah, that would be a shit kicker," Brody said, trying to hang onto the jargon Sarina had gone over with him. Kids today talked so damn weird. "So you just ship everything east and forget about the market that's just waiting for you out west?"

"Well now," Mike said with a smile. "I didn't say we were just sitting back, now did I?"

"Well, no."

"It's taken a while now," Mike explained. "But we're hoping that by pooling our resources, we can run a track of properties through the Delta region and make a safe way through that area where humans can travel without the threat that may or may not actually exist out that way. Considering no one's ever seen a werewolf and brought back proof, it's all still just a myth. Still, I'd rather be safe than sorry. It's not like we can take the fight to them or anything. And who knows, maybe they'll decide they like what we're selling. It'd be nice to score some more home town customers, you know?"

"I do," Brody said. So, if what he'd learned tonight meant anything, it wasn't war these people wanted. It was buyers and lots of them. The unfortunate part was that they needed safe passage past the New Delta region. Brody thought it would be best not to increase the human traffic into their wolf dominated region. Convincing a bunch of money hungry young adults that bypassing the region was the way to go wasn't going to be nearly as easy as just kicking their asses in a war. Brody knew though that he had to do everything in his power to make peace with these people. Helping them with their problem seemed the smoothest way to do that. At the same time, he could help convince them to go around the wolves habitat.

"Awesome, man." Brody nearly died when Mike picked him up in a bear hug. If he hadn't been inhibited by Amanda's potion, he'd probably have killed Mike just to save himself the trouble. Wouldn't that have been a bitch?

"What in the hell could be taking this long?" Sarina fumed, pacing in her parents' living room. Having just put the twins down for a nap, she needed a moment to vent. "It's been nearly two weeks and there's been absolutely no word from Brody about anything he's found out, or not found out."

"Sweetheart, you have to be patient and give Brody time." said Amanda

"I have!" she seethed. Sighing, Sarina ran a hand through her dark hair. "Oh, Mama. I'm frustrated that everyone here is so happy while I'm miserable."

"Is that the way you see it?" Amanda said, smiling. "Because I see a vigilant and diligent wife who loves her husband and simply wants everything to return to normal for once in her complicated life."

"Have I mentioned you're my favorite?" Sarina said, returning the smile.

"I remember feeling much the same way as you when your father and I met. I'd gone from this comfortable co-ed to a werewolf and witch nearly over night. I'd been all but told I'd have to marry Romeo, whether or not I liked it, if I wanted to stay alive and nothing felt as if it was any of my choice.

"Even the first time I slept with him, as much as I chose to do it, the decision still didn't feel completely mine. I had all this hanging over my head and no one to talk to about it. My parents were dead and these people who kept demanding my cooperation weren't any more familiar to me than Adam from the garden."

"I have to admit, I don't often think about how hard it must have been for you, going through all of that alone."

"Alone?" Amanda scoffed. "I couldn't have been less alone if I'd tried. Someone was always checking on me, asking me how I was doing, and demanding answers from me I wasn't even sure I could comprehend. And much like you I suffered through my own kidnapping. Of course, I did meet your Aunt Penelope that way, but still, I'd have liked a say in the matter."

"Will you tell me the story?"

Sarina sat at her mother's feet, smiling when Shawna and Gina came to sit with them as well. Newly married, Gina and Turk would soon be heading to a different part of the world for a while, but Sarina knew they'd eventually return here and become an official part of the Delta pack.

"It all started when I was contacted by my Aunt Mabel's lawyer to tell me that my only living relative, whom I knew absolutely nothing about, had passed away; leaving me her entire estate."

Amanda retold the tale of how she and Romeo had come to be the rulers of the Delta pack and Sarina sighed as she listened, knowing just how much love she and Brody had, because she'd seen it in her parents first. Still, when she went home, she went without her mate and that was the hardest thing she'd ever done. If she'd ever wanted a glimpse of what life would be like without Brody, she'd gotten that glimpse and it wasn't a life she would ever like to have.

Sarina tucked her boys into bed with warm kisses and bedtime stories about a werewolf who saved his people from war, then she turned out the lights and sought the solitude of her bedroom. She'd tried in the past several days to reach out to Brody in her mind, but the potion that made him mostly human, must have blocked his ability to hear her as well. Every message she sent out, never received an answer.

She showered and tucked herself in for the night, choosing the center of the bed so she'd sleep at least partially where Brody lay when he slept. Tucking her hand under his pillow, Sarina fell quickly asleep, but rest eluded her. In sleep, Sarina dreamed of Brody and what he must be experiencing in the human world.

"You're not going to want to build a road that way," Brody said to a broad, muscular man. Nearly as tall as her mate, the man seemed kind, but Sarina couldn't help sense the tinge of anger that boiled beneath the surface of his skin.

"Why?" the man asked, his curious eyes roaming over a pretty blonde who stood close to him.

"Trust me, friend. There are some things you don't know about that area. Weird shit happens around that place and it's not somewhere you're going to want to risk your stock."

"What sort of weird shit?"

"The sort that people only whisper about because there's never any proof," Brody said, downing the last of what looked like beer.

"Oh yeah?" the man snickered. "And how exactly do you know this?"

"I've seen it," Brody said, smiling. "I'm short of details, for obvious reasons. But I've seen what lurks around that area and trust me, you don't want to go there."

"Then find me a way around and I'll make it worth your while."

"Deal," Brody replied confidently. "You'll need to give me some time to work it out, but I'll make sure you have a relatively safe and easy way to get those to the people who want them. My fee is twenty-five percent."

The man nearly spit his beer out. "Twenty-five? I can't do more than fifteen without cutting into my own profit."

"Well," Brody said with a sinister smile. "Just think about how fast you'll recoup the missing ten percent when you can reach all the way to the west coast. Certainly the short term loss is worth the long term gain."

"Maybe," the guy said. "I'll think about it. Let me know when you've got a plan and what you need to get started."

It was the wee hours of the morning, when the moon's light still shone bright in the sky, as Sarina brewed herself a cup of coffee. She normally preferred tea, but with Brody gone, she found herself longing for him so badly that the smell and taste of coffee soothed her soul some. What the hell was Brody doing over there?

Was he really trying to set up a way around the New Delta area for humans to traffic drugs? Was that the sort of man she was married to? Werewolf or not, her kind had manners and morals, morals Brody obviously didn't share. She needed to talk to her parents and fast. As soon as the boys woke up, Sarina grabbed granola bars and juice and packed them up for a trip up the hill.

"Sarina?" said Shawna when she opened the door. Clearly she'd just woken up and was surprised to see the sister who'd just left the night before. "Everything okay?"

"I hope so," she said. "Where are Mom and Dad?"

"In the kitchen, probably."

Sarina headed toward the kitchen feeling better when she heard her parents' voices.

"Sarina, what's wrong?"

She always loved the way her parents could tell, with just a look, that something wasn't right.

"I had a dream about Brody last night. I think he's trying to find a way around the New Delta area so that the humans can traffic drugs to the west without coming through here."

Sarina felt as if she had two heads the way her parents looked at her.

"I know it sounds crazy," she rushed on. "But I can't shake the feeling that whatever trouble we could be potentially facing, it's not so much a physical as it is that which will battle every area of our lives."

"Alright," Romeo said. "Then we need to call Brody back and figure out what's going on. Then we'll reassess whether or not we can send him back."

Brody woke from a nightmare the next morning and cursed the hangover that pummeled in his head, like a battering ram jackhammer. He could have set a clock by it, the throbbing was so consistent. Mixing up a cocktail of orange juice and pain killers, Brody choked it down and hoped he'd be able to see straight within the hour.

After a long shower, he felt somewhat better and began to dress for his next visit. He needed to figure out who the man in the vision was and track down his descendants. He made it to the library without dying and figured that was as good as it was going to get today.

"May I help you?" asked an elderly librarian.

"I'd like the archives room, please," said Brody.

"Sure, Sonya will be able to help you with anything you might need."

"Thank you," Brody replied before heading downstairs. For a small town, the library was huge and when he hit the landing of the staircase, Brody knew why. Above the passageway to the archives room a plaque read: *In Memory of Mr. C. Henry and Mrs. Elena Whittaker.* Perhaps C. Henry Whittaker was a descendant of the man in the vision, Brody thought to himself.

He entered into the secluded room and had to admit that for archives, it was pretty nice. Neat and organized, much like Sarina preferred, it wouldn't be hard this way to find what he was looking for.

"May I help you?"

Brody turned to find a stunning woman standing close by. Not so long ago he would have thought it a shame that a woman like her was stuck in a place like this so many hours of the day. Now though, his thought centered on his job and the incredible woman waiting for him at home. She'd been all it took to turn him into a family man.

"Um, yes. I need to know if there's any record of a double murder happening somewhere around here. It was quite a long time ago so I'm not sure there's any record of it, to be honest."

"Well, if we can narrow down the time, that would help a lot."

"I'm guessing at least a hundred years ago, maybe even more?"

"Alright," the young woman said. "I'm Michelle by the way. Most people just call me Chelle for short. We'll start with nineteen hundred and work our way up from there. Hopefully we'll canvass what you're looking for."

Brody sat down at the microfiche machine as Chelle brought him pile after pile of slides. By lunch he was nearly cross-eyed and blind from reading so much. He had found, though, some interesting information. It seems C. Henry Whittaker was married to Elena Michelle Walker. Ms. Walker, before she married, had a father, one Elijah David Morris-Walker. Elijah's mother was none other than Martha Amanda Walker. She'd married Jackson Walker and they'd had a baby they named Abigail. Later, after their deaths, it seemed Jackson had been able to move on and he married Lena Matthews. It seemed that, while they never had children, they lived out their days together. With no divorce on record, their marriage lasted some fifty-six years, only ending because Jackson died of natural causes at the age of one hundred and one.

The story that made the town paper way back when stated that Jackson Walker had returned home after a night of drinking to find his wife and daughter torn to shreds by a huge dog-like beast. Brody had to wonder about what Amanda had been told, if anything, about her great-grandfather, Elijah. Elijah grew up and dropped his name to Elijah David Walker. His son, Adam Scott Walker married a beautiful woman named

Scarlett. Their children Mabel and Joshua Walker became Amanda Walker's aunt and father.

"Thank you," Brody said as he left the archives room. He headed back to his room and packed. The sooner he got home with this information, the better. The full moon would come that night and Brody drank one of the vials to keep himself from changing. It'd mean another month of being just this side of werewolf, but it couldn't be avoided. He couldn't risk the change when he was still among this many humans.

Chapter Nine

Sarina knew almost instantly upon waking that Brody was headed home. Her heart raced and everything seemed brighter as the love she felt for him swamped her. She rushed through a shower and dressed the boys quickly. When she finished, she drove them up to her parents.

"Nana!" little Brody squealed when he saw Amanda step onto the porch.

"Papa!" Jedidiah yelled, holding out his hands and running haphazardly toward Romeo on the porch.

"I came to see if you'd like to watch them for a couple hours? I think Brody's on his way home and I'd like to have some time to cook and clean before he arrives."

"Alright," Amanda smiled. "I'm glad your family will be whole again."

"Me too," Sarina squealed as she nearly bounced back to her car. She cooked Brody's favorite meal and cleaned the house spotless before decorating the bathroom and their bedroom with flowers and candles she'd light once she saw him, knew he was safe and sound. By the time nightfall hit, Sarina felt the

disappointment seep into her bones. She'd thought with
absolute belief that he'd be home today and now that he
wasn't, she brought her boys back home, fighting the
tears that threatened to undo her.

"When Daddy be home?" little Brody asked as she
tucked him into his bed. Now that they were two,
Sarina and Brody had converted the guest bedroom, at
the opposite end of the hall, into a toddler room that
screamed *boy*.

"Oh sweetheart," Sarina cooed. "I wish I knew."
She kissed both of her boys, shut off their light and
slipped out, leaving the door open just a crack so she
could hear them if they woke up. She went into the
bathroom and started to pick up the candles and petals
she'd set out, feeling her heart sink even lower than it
already had.

"Now why would a man stand up a beautiful
woman like you?" Sarina nearly dropped the candles in
her hands when she turned around to see Brody
standing in the doorway. Unable to contain the smile
that filled her soul, Sarina hurriedly placed the candles
in the closest sink and ran to her mate, jumping into his
arms.

Braced for her, Brody chuckled when she filled his
arms. But that didn't stop him from burying his face in
her hair and inhaling her scent. God he'd missed her,
missed this. Pulling back he pressed a hard kiss to her
waiting lips before he let her go.

"I thought maybe I'd misjudged your home coming.
It took you a long time to get here."

"There are things I need to tell your parents, everyone really. But it can wait until morning," Brody said. Taking a lighter from his pocket, Brody grabbed Sarina's hand and walked her toward their room. He took his time lighting the candles she'd set out and then he took his time loving the mate he'd had to leave behind. He swore he'd never do that again. It was a promise he meant to keep.

The following morning, Brody, Sarina and the twins headed out for the Traverse mansion. They were welcomed with much love and admiration as Brody was peppered with a million questions.

"Let them come in and sit down!" Romeo shouted above the din in the foyer.

Slowly everyone made a way for Brody and Sarina to enter the kitchen and sit down. The twins were scooped up by Gina and Shawna who enjoyed them immensely as everyone met in the family gathering spot. Whatever the situation or problem, the Walker-Traverse kitchen was where everyone gathered to learn the results.

"So," Romeo said with a smile. "Tell us what we're all dying to know. No pun intended."

"Well, let me first say that humans are as unique and varied as we are. They have differences of opinions and for the most part aren't all that different from us, except for the whole full moon werewolf part." Everyone chuckled. Continuing Brody added, "I searched the library archives and came across an article that talked about a double murder of a woman and baby girl. Turns out the woman's name was Martha Amanda Walker and her daughter's name was Abigail. She was married to a man named Jackson Walker who eventually remarried and lived with his wife Lena Matthews in a cottage by the sea. They never had children and after nearly sixty years together, both died within months of each other.

Martha had a son from a previous marriage named Elijah. When he hit puberty, the change came over him and he killed his mother and baby sister. Jackson had no idea it was Elijah who'd done the killing. Elijah grew up and changed his name from Elijah David Morris-Walker to Elijah David Walker. He married a beautiful woman and had a son and daughter. His son, Adam Scott Walker married a pretty brunette named Scarlett and they had two children; Mabel Annabel Walker and Joshua Jackson Walker. Joshua married a pretty woman named Maureen and they had a lovely daughter named—"

"Amanda Michelle Walker," Amanda whispered, tears brimming in her eyes. Without another word she turned and left the kitchen.

Sarina moved to go after her mother, but she felt Romeo's hand on her arm.

"She'll need to sit with it awhile before she can talk about it," he said.

Sarina smiled her understanding, but her heart hurt for her mother. Later when everyone had gone their separate ways, Sarina headed for her parents' room, not surprised when she didn't find her mother there. She took the stairs that led to the special room her mother had made and knocked lightly.

"Come in," her mother said, her voice strained with tears.

"Mama?" Sarina said as she stepped into a room full of deep purples and blues.

"You'll have to forgive me. I'm terrible company."

"I don't mind," Sarina replied. "I came to see if you're okay."

"I thought for a long time that I had moved past my parents' deaths, that their hurt and pain were tucked away where they couldn't rule me anymore. Today I learned differently."

"There's no shame in that, Mama."

"No," Amanda said with a sad smile. "No shame. But that doesn't stop the grief… grief I thought I'd gotten past by now."

"Well, you certainly didn't expect you'd find out your great-grandfather was the werewolf who killed what turned out to be your great-great-grandmother and his half-sister."

"I didn't know anything about anything," Amanda said. "My father and mother tried to give me a normal life, even though they knew I was headed here. They knew I'd turn twenty-four and come into season; that

I'd be hunted by our kind for breeding rights; that I'd learn of my powers. Why did everyone I know try so damn hard to keep it all from me?"

"Maybe they hoped it'd help you cope once you found out. Or maybe they were hoping you'd never have to know and would continue to live a normal life."

"But they must have known that Aunt Mabel left me her estate right?"

"Not if she did it after they were killed."

"Point taken," Amanda said with a sigh. "I just wish I knew more, had more answers."

"Maybe the answers you have now are enough."

"How so?"

"Well," Sarina said, filling the room with warm pinks and hues of amber, her calm, comforting colors. "Maybe knowing who the werewolf was, where you came from, will help you put some of your past to rest. Do you think you can put the cabin behind you now?"

"I'm not sure… maybe. I have to admit it was quite a shock to hear Brody's report. My great-grandfather being responsible for those deaths brings home why your father taught me to satisfy my need with cattle or livestock blood. We can't live in peace with humans if we're constantly tempted by them."

"True," Sarina said with sad smile to match her mother's. "I was a bit shocked when Brody told me that his pack hunted humans. It was Dad who taught him and his pack to rely on animals, mainly cows and wild game. The whole point about living and working with humans though, makes a lot of sense. While we may not willingly seek them out, we can't really avoid them at every turn either."

"Have I ever told you that I like the way you think?" Amanda said.

"I get it from my mother," Sarina said with a wink.

"She must be an amazing woman."

"I'll be sure to tell her so," Sarina said, chuckling. "Would you like to go get some pie? Shawna made an apple pie that's to die for. She's going to make some wolf a very, very happy man someday."

"Someday soon," Amanda pouted. "All my chicks are fleeing the coop."

"Not fleeing, Mama," Sarina replied. She threaded her arm through her mother's and together they left the isolation of the room and headed upstairs. "Just changing addresses. And just think… the sooner she finds a mate, the more likely you are to have more grandchildren."

"You are your mother's daughter."

The next few days passed normally with lots of sunshine and love. Brody and Sarina took the boys to see *Hotel Transylvania 2*, which the twins couldn't stop jabbering about.

"We-wolf, Dad!" little Brody screamed, bouncing up and down in his seat while he was being buckled in.

"You're right, buddy. There was a werewolf," Brody said chuckling at the young boy.

"I doggy," Jedidiah added with a big, toothy smile.

Sarina smiled. "You like the doggy? Did you know that not everyone is a doggy?"

"That's true," Brody added, picking up the conversation as he slipped behind the wheel. Once Sarina was in and buckled, he continued. "Gina's mommy and daddy are werewolves, but Gina won't be."

"Gina!" little Brody squealed, obviously delighted by the thought of his mother's cousin. Because she was so very special, Gina had a special place in both little Brody and Jedidiah's hearts.

"Gina! Gina!" the boys chanted in unison.

"We go home and see Gina, Mommy?" asked little Brody.

"Not tonight," Sarina said. "She and Turk are going to head into the town that Daddy went to. We're going to see if we can't figure out a way to help the humans so they don't have as many dangerous run-ins with our kind, especially on the full moon."

"We no longer hunt humans" Brody said. "Because sometimes, for peace, it's better to go against what you've been taught, even what seems natural."

"Humans," Jedidiah giggled as he and Brody Jr. yawned, indicating they were both tuckered out.

"Animals," Sarina corrected. "When your first change comes, we'll be ready to teach you both how things are done. And you'll learn the tradition of the Traverse clan, which is very, very old and time-honored."

"Okay," the twins said in unison. "We go home, get food?"

"Sounds like a plan," Brody said, chuckling to himself.

Brody agreed to head back to Brownsville, the town that was fifty miles outside of the New Delta area, to help the humans who lived there deal with their little problem. Another goodbye to his family wasn't possible and he'd promised not to leave them behind this time. So, with Amanda and Romeo's blessing, Sarina and the twins went along this time.

Three quarters of the way there, Romeo dropped all four of them off with kisses, hugs and well-wishes. "Y'all take care of each other. We'll see you again soon."

"Will do, Dad," said Brody.

Romeo looked nearly as shocked to hear the word escape Brody's lips, as the man himself was to say it. With a salute, again, the four took off and headed toward town. Kale Pearson, the old man who'd picked Brody up the first time, happened by this time, as well.

"Well, sonny, look at what you picked up since the last time I saw you."

"Last time I was foolish enough to leave them behind. Swore I wouldn't do that again," Brody said with a grin, setting his hand comfortably over Sarina's bare knee. The hold man noticed, clearing his throat as if the gesture made him slightly uncomfortable.

"Can't say I blame you," Kale chuckled. "You've got yourself one fine family."

"Wouldn't have it any other way," Brody agreed.

"So how long you think you're staying this time?"

"I can't say," Brody said, evading a direct answer. "My work takes me all over so I'm never in one place for any length of time, but hopefully we'll be here long enough to at least see some sights."

"Ain't much to see in Brownsville to be honest, but if you're into historical stuff you might like the war reenactments they do here."

"Really? They do that here?"

"Yeah, those history buffs gotta have somethin' to do when they get bored. If they didn't do this they'd be sitting in their living rooms huffin' and puffin' about their opinions and some such shit."

Brody laughed, liking Kale Pearson more and more the longer he spent in his company. "You're absolutely right," he agreed. "Maybe we'll check that out while we're here."

Brody and Sarina were dropped off with the twins in front of the little bed and breakfast Brody had used the first time he'd stayed in town.

"This place is beautiful," Sarina said, smiling. "Too bad we couldn't have gone here for a honeymoon."

"Who says we can't?" Brody winked. "The twins are old enough to stay over with your parents and I for one have been dying to get away."

"Really?" Sarina said, shocked. "I just… I thought you were sort of married to New Delta and the pack, especially."

"I'm married to you, love. You and the boys are my biggest concern and reward. It's you I put all my energy into. If it means I help the pack in the process so be it. Other than that all I want is to spend every moment I can with you and the boys."

"Well aren't you sweet today." Sarina gave a twinkling smile. Leaning over, she kissed him, a kiss that promised more once the boys went down for a nap.

"You know it, babe," said Brody.

<<◇>>

"Think they've gotten anywhere?"

"I don't know," Romeo said, addressing Amanda's question. "We'll know when they return. Whatever the results, I'm certain Brody and Sarina can resolve any problem that arises. The only issue will be if they run out of vials. They'd have to return for more, which would slow things down, but not derail them."

"I'm sure you're right," Amanda said, smiling. "Still, I can't help but be a little anxious."

"Try to relax, darling. It's only been two weeks. Just because Brody came back earlier than we thought he might, doesn't mean things will go that quickly this time."

"Right," Amanda agreed. Still, she couldn't sleep and she couldn't shake the gut feeling that things weren't as settled as she'd hoped. With no one to keep tabs on her this time around, Amanda stepped off her front porch and headed into the woods during those predawn hours when her side of the earth was still sleeping. She'd memorized her way to the cabin and knew exactly when to stop as she'd marked a tree.

"Stop!" she heard in a booming voice. "Step no further Amanda Walker."

"Who are you?" she asked, her voice quavering.

"I am she who was killed here so long ago."

Amanda watched as a woman appeared to her. Long, flowing, chestnut hair, her robe still showed the stains where she'd been mauled by Elijah Walker.

"You are the bloodline of the thing that killed me and therefore stricken from seeing this sacred place."

"But why? Elijah didn't know how to control what he was, because no one was there to help him during that first change."

"Elijah?" the woman said, her face clearly showing the shock of the information. "My Elijah did this?"

"He didn't know any better," Amanda said as tears filled her eyes. "The change came over him so quickly that he couldn't have controlled it, no matter how he may have wanted to." Amanda watched as the woman paced around the area where the cabin stood, as if she was trying to understand this new information.

Suddenly the cabin materialized and Amanda sighed when she saw the condition of the place. "May I restore the cabin?"

"What?" the woman asked, her pale, see-through blue eyes burdened by the story she carried.

"I'd like to, with your permission of course, restore this cabin and put up a marker for you and your daughter. You want your story told and I understand that. It's part of why oral and written tradition is so important to my kind."

"Why would a werewolf care about this place, let alone my story?"

"Because I'm more than just a werewolf," Amanda said, slightly surprised by the pride that filled her with the admission. "I'm a witch. But more than that, I'm a mother, with children of my own, one who died in these very woods. I know the importance of remembering and I'd like for my kin to remember you and your story, the story of your daughter and your son."

Amanda watched a little girl appear beside her mother and she smiled, lowering herself to Abigail's height.

"Hello Abigail," said Amanda.

The little girl, a near mirror image of her mother, smiled and waved. She looked to be about two, the age she was when her half-brother took her life.

"I have grandsons who are about your age, twins to boot. Would it be okay if I rebuilt this place to look better and put up a stone for you and your mama and brother?"

The little girl shook her head vigorously, looking up at her mother and grinning. Amanda stood again and gasped in shock when the woman reached out and touched her face. "Thank you," she said as a tear slid down her cheek. "We can rest now."

Chapter Ten

Brody and Sarina met with Camille and Mike about planning a way around the Delta region. It would take some more detailed work and plans, schematics and blueprints would have to be drawn up, but Brody offered manpower and supplies if Mike agreed to steer clear of the New Delta.

"We can make this work," Mike said, smiling. "It's brilliant."

"Glad you like it," Brody replied with an undertone of relief. "So, give me a couple of weeks to get some shit together and we'll come back this way with everything we need to get started. Don't get me wrong, it's going to take at least six months to really get you moving, but it'll be worth it in the long run."

"You got it," Mike said, shaking Brody's hand. "And if there's anything I can do for you in the meantime, just let me know."

"I will," Brody agreed.

He and Sarina took their twins home, updated Romeo and Amanda, tucked their twins into the Traverse mansion, and headed back to Brownsville with over a hundred workers. Most would need to return during their agreed upon week off each month, to make the change without alerting the human citizens who lived in the town, but other than that, work would continue non-stop with two crews of fifty working night and day to finish what Mike and Camille needed to expand west without entering the New Delta territory.

Some time went by before Brody and Sarina were able to make it home for any length of time and Amanda knew not only did they need to know about the cabin and everything else, they also needed to see their sons and enjoy some serious comfort food. "I'm starving!" Sarina giggled as she stuffed her face with a warm biscuit straight from the oven, smothered with butter and honey. "Don't ever send me away again without food," she begged.

"It's a promise," Amanda said with a smile. "Alright everyone, if you'll grab a seat, I need to go over some changes that have taken place now that Brody and Sarina are home."

"Unable to sleep a while back, I took a trip into the woods to visit the cabin. Thanks to the information Brody brought back from Brownsville, I was able to draw out the ghosts of both Mrs. Walker and her daughter, Abigail."

"Really?" Sarina asked, scooting forward in her chair. "What happened?"

"I explained that Elijah didn't know what to do when the change came over him. I told her that with no one there to explain things, to buoy that experience, Elijah would only have done what was natural and instinctive to the werewolf he became."

"What did she say?" The way everyone waited, it seemed everyone wanted to know with equal anxiousness. Amanda smiled.

"She thanked me and gave me permission to restore the cabin to its former glory. I'm also going to put up a marker for Mrs. Walker, her young daughter Abigail, and Elijah as well."

"Oh Mama, that's wonderful."

"I know." Amanda gave a thoughtful nod.

With the construction project in Brownsville well underway and Brody and Sarina moving back and forth between the town and home, things were moving along smoothly. Relations with the humans had never been better and the future looked very nice.

Amanda, along with many of the immediate Traverse clan had gotten together to draw blueprints of the original structure of the Walker cabin. Construction commenced on a Wednesday morning that dawned bright and wonderful. As new floors were put down, a peace settled over Amanda for the first time in years. The humans didn't want to start a war with the werewolves. In fact, they seemed to want to ignore their existence all together. It was a solution that suited Romeo and Amanda perfectly.

"So, how goes the cabin?" Romeo asked when he dropped by to meet Amanda for lunch.

"It's incredible," Amanda beamed. "I can't believe how beautiful this place is."

"I never realized how dark the woods were before now," he said. "When the work started here, especially after that stone went up, this whole place just brightened up. We should think about building some housing out here for wolves that like this sort of setup."

"That's a fantastic idea," Amanda said, looking her mate in the eyes. "I know several of our pack's members would love to reside in these woods."

"Then we'll start getting on that," he said with a smile. "Give me a list of names and I'll see if I can't scrape together a team to get started."

"Brody and Sarina for starters."

"Seriously?"

"Absolutely. Sarina loves these woods and from the stories she told me of their mating, I'm pretty sure Brody would acclimate well to this area. Not to mention, they can keep an eye on everyone out here and watch over this cabin."

"I think Elijah, Penelope, and Jeremiah should move out here too."

"Really?" asked Amanda.

"Why not? My brother has a knack for nature. I also think they should live here, in the cabin."

"Romeo I—"

"This place needs people again, babe," Romeo said, explaining his point. "I know its sacred ground and who better to reside here than a werewolf and a Radiant? Who better to respect the history of this place? You know Eli and Pen would care for this place, more than it just being a home."

"We'd be honored," Elijah said, walking over with Penelope and Jeremiah in tow.

"You're still as nosy as ever," Romeo joked. He gave Elijah a light punch in the arm before he settled them on a picnic table close to the construction site.

"True," he replied with a cocky smile. "However, Pen has two conditions. One, flower beds. She wants to put flowers here. She also wants to keep the picnic table. She said we should have lunch here as often as possible."

"I think that can be arranged," Romeo agreed.

"How are things coming along in Brownsville?"

"Well," Brody said as he and Romeo scouted the land in the woods. "We just received clearance from the towns we'll be moving through that the main road is a go. If we keep up this schedule, we should finish well ahead of our original deadline. With the two alternating crews, the work is really moving along smoothly. Mike and Camille, the two humans we deal with most often, have been incredible and they have a great work ethic. If it works to keep increased human traffic out of New Delta; that's what I'm after."

"Excellent," Romeo said, surveying a beautiful plot of land that had a stream running through it. "Now, since we're out here anyways, why not pick a nice plot of land to raise my grandsons on."

"Your daughter is partial to streams," Brody replied, nodding toward the plot Romeo had been eyeing. "Although we're going to need to adjust our housing plans some."

"Oh?" Romeo questioned.

"We'll need at least four bedrooms and plenty of workable yard space, for when the children get older."

"The boys will make do with whatever you have," Romeo chuckled.

"Yes, but I'm afraid their little sister may drive them out of their minds if we don't give them enough—"

"Did you say little sister?"

"I did, indeed," Brody said, smiling.

"Well shit," Romeo beamed with happiness. "Does Amanda know?"

"She will soon if she doesn't already."

Just as Brody was finishing his sentence, Romeo winced as Amanda's voice squealed through his mind. *We're having a granddaughter!*

"I'm pretty sure she knows now," Romeo said, holding his hands to his temples to block some of Amanda's excitement.

Epilogue

As the months passed, fourteen homes were built in the woods, each with a ten acre allotment of yard space that each family was responsible for. Brody and Sarina had decided that perhaps five bedrooms would do, just in case the baby girl turned into two baby girls or a split decision.

The cabin had been torn down to the original framework which was used to plank out for new, but historical flooring. In its place, a beautiful and brand new three bedroom cabin stood, stately and lovely. The remembrance rock Amanda had placed close to the cabin read:

To the memories of Martha Morris-Walker, Abigail Walker and Elijah David Morris-Walker. May they all rest in peace, knowing their lives mattered to those they left behind. Their story will never die as long as we live.

Amanda had included an entire journal about the experience and the story of Martha, Abigail, and Elijah.

"It's a lovely spot," Penelope said as she sat with Amanda on the picnic table, enjoying a mojito.

"Yes it is." She smiled her agreement.

"Do you think if they're really resting now?"

"I would think so," Amanda assured her. "Wouldn't you, if you'd fought like the dickens to conceal a place like this for that many years? I could almost feel the relief pumping off of her when I told her about Elijah. She needed to know and all this time no one had ever taken the time to tell her."

"You did."

"I just… I couldn't let it go. I couldn't turn and run away from something like that."

"That's why it waited for you. Out of all those journal entries, the secrets in your family needed to come out the way they did. It all led you to this, to these moments."

"I couldn't agree more," Amanda said.

"Good," Penelope replied. "Now help me get down so we can go harass Sarina about the baby."

"She'll kill us if we wake that angel," Amanda warned.

"Yeah well, she'd have to catch us first and no offense to your progeny, but I'm betting she's not up to par just yet."

"Probably not, but you're going in first."

"Bitch." Penelope chuckled.

"Ditto." Amanda laughed in return.

<<<>>>

Abigail Martha Duscene was the beautiful image of her mother, all dark hair and eyes. She was slight, small and petite. It was easy to see that while Brody loved his sons, little Abigail had her daddy wrapped around her finger. Already Brody had nearly bitten the heads off of two gardeners who'd stopped by to replant some flowers and accidentally woke his sleeping angel from her nap.

"I can't get over her," Sarina said with a sigh, handing the sleeping bundle to Penelope.

"There's no need to," her aunt said with a smile. "She's beyond perfect and truth be told, she makes me want a little girl with Elijah."

"And what does he say when you mention that?"

"He all but curses me to no end." Penelope laughed. "No, we're done with offspring. But that doesn't mean a girl can't want."

"So how are you and Uncle Elijah adjusting to the new cabin?"

"It's familiar, in a weird, almost science fiction sort of way. But there's so much love there, I can only suspect that it was the same for the Walkers before Elijah turned."

"I think that's a fair assumption," Amanda nodded. "When I talked with Martha and Abigail, you could tell they had loved each other. While Jackson and Elijah hadn't shown their faces, I could feel them near. I can only hope they settled things between them in the afterlife. It's terrible to leave things unsaid here, let alone after you pass over."

"I'm sure they did," Penelope said. "Still, even if not, we've put their demons away and they're both resting now. There's a serious level of peace in these woods now.

"True," Amanda agreed. "I can attest that a peace like that wasn't present even six months ago, not that I can believe we've been at this whole thing that long."

"Will you be going back to Brownsville anytime soon?" Penelope asked of Sarina.

"Not anytime soon," she stated. "Brody has everything well under control and while I miss him terribly when he's gone, I know that I'm needed here now. With our home finally finished, I can focus on raising our children in an environment that will love and accept the changes that Elijah couldn't handle in himself. I know that our pack will be there even if Brody and I can't be. That's important to me."

"You're damn right we'll be here," Amanda said, reaching out to cover Sarina's hand. "No matter what happens in the future, the Delta pack will always take care of its own, no matter how small the pack member. Has your dad marked her yet?"

"We're going to do it tonight, once Brody gets back."

"Sounds good, doll. I can get the details from your father. I'd like to be here when he brings her officially into the pack."

"Sounds like a plan, Mama. How are Brandt and Carly doing?"

"They're loving their new home," Amanda said. "Carly thinks she wants to hire you to decorate for her. She said she loved what you did, but she's got some different color palates in mind."

"I can't blame her, setting your own mark on a home is a ritual for us women."

"That's true," Amanda laughed. "Lord knows I drove your father crazy during those first few years of our marriage trying to figure out how I wanted to do the decorating around our home. My aunt, God love her, wasn't the most cheerful woman. I guess maybe dark colors and shades of shadow were all the rage during her time, but whenever I stepped into that mansion, before we redid it, I'd get depressed."

"Werewolves can suffer from depression?" Sarina asked, a chuckle on the tip of her tongue.

"Go ahead and laugh," said Amanda, smiling. "But at the time, I barely knew what a werewolf was, let alone that I was one."

"I bet Aunt Mabel was so cool."

"She was definitely a forward thinker."

Later that night, when the whole Walker-Traverse-Duscene family could pile into the Duscene great room, Romeo inducted little Abigail Martha into the pack. It was the official welcoming for their newest member and everyone toasted the little girl's arrival and the future she represented.

After everyone headed home, Sarina, tucked herself into bed with Abigail, smiled at Brody when he climbed in to join them.

"She's beautiful," Brody whispered, placing a feather light kiss on his new daughter's forehead.

"Yes she is." Sarina smiled.

"She must take after her mother," he said softly.

"I'm sure she does," Sarina gently replied.

"Maybe I'll tell her so one day."

"I'm sure she'd like to hear that."

He kissed her then, knowing that whatever life threw at them and wherever they went from there, they'd go together, stronger in the knowledge that their lives had infinite meaning and value, as long as, they loved and were loved in return.

-The End-

If you enjoyed this title, I would appreciate your leaving a review of the book. Good reviews encourage an author to write as well as help books to sell. Good reviews can be just a few short sentences describing what you liked about the book without having a spoiler. If you could spend 30 seconds writing a review, I would appreciate it: you can review this title right now at your favorite retailer.

Here is a preview of **another story** you may also enjoy:

Alpha Packed: A BBW Paranormal Shifter Romance - Book 1

THIS WAS a huge mistake. Darlene should have known better, but in utter and total desperation, she agreed to this date. Now the guy in front of her—what was his name again? Steve? Mike? She couldn't even remember now—had been talking non-stop about pro wrestling. But not even actual real wrestling. The stuff that was fake and basically just soap operas with some terrible phony fights thrown in.

"So then the Ice Cube challenged The Man to a battle!"

"Wow, really?" Darlene replied, feigning interest on every possible level.

This was her mistake. She had been spending way too much time at home lately, curled up on the couch, binge watching reality television shows because they made her feel better about her boring life. Darlene would leave for work in the mornings, do eight hours at a boring local bookstore, come home, eat and watch TV. She also stayed up far later than any normal human should, which resulted in limited forms of social communication.

That was how Darlene ended up on some free dating website. She deleted most of the messages she got. They were mostly from guys who seemed to think of her as a sexual fetish instead of an actual human being. Getting messages from guys who were into her being overweight made her feel uncomfortable. Darlene either got disgusted looks or sexual lust over her size.

Both sucked. She had been about to delete her page for good when a guy who appeared to be normal messaged her. He hadn't made any gross comments about her size and even made her laugh once or twice with his messages. It had been eight months since her last relationship blew up in her face. *Why not try something different?* She decided to accept his date.

The guy was so boring that Darlene wished the restaurant would go up in flames so she could flee. She was flipping through her options on how to end the date early when he finally pushed his plate away.

"That was delicious," he said.

"Oh yeah. It was great," Darlene lied, thinking the potatoes were too dry for her liking.

The check came and the guy—what was his name!—made an effort to search for his wallet. *Oh here we go...*

"Oh man. I forgot my wallet at home!" he said with fake surprise.

"Yeah, yeah, I got it," she mumbled, slamming her debit card on the table.

It didn't take a genius to figure out this asshole had asked her out to throw her what he thought was a "pity date" and get a free meal out of her. He would probably go home to all his idiot friends and talk about how he gave the fat girl a date because he was just so nice. Darlene felt like punching him in the face.

She paid, and they walked out of the restaurant in silence. He escorted her to her car and then glanced around, as if checking so that no one could see him, before he tried to kiss her.

"Yeah," Darlene lifted up her hand to block him, "I don't think so. Thanks for nothing though, seriously."

The man scowled and before he could say something back, Darlene got into her car. She pulled out of the parking lot as quickly as she could, wanting to forget the entire terrible date.

What a mistake. What an absolute mistake. Not even just the date. The last couple years of her life had been a huge mistake. She wished she could travel back in time and re-do everything. The first thing she'd do would be to say a resounding *no* when Austin proposed to her.

Darlene pulled into her apartment complex five minutes later. She had picked a nearby restaurant so she could make a quick escape home if needed. She walked up to the second floor. The couple by the stairwell was fighting again. They were constantly screaming at each other over everything. Some nights, Darlene wanted to yell back at them to just break up. Other times, she wanted to tell them to make it work, because being alone was terrible.

She opened the front door of her apartment and glanced around. Her computer was on in one corner, and a few blankets were thrown on the couch for maximum comfort for those times when she drowned herself in ice cream and terrible reality shows.

Everything else was clean though. Darlene couldn't stand her apartment being messy or dirty. She wanted it to be perfect, as if she could make her apartment look like how she didn't feel.

Darlene yanked off her high heels and plopped down in front of her computer. She deleted the online dating profile and stared out the window. That was it — she was going to become a hermit. Well, as much of a hermit as one can be if they still had to go to work and grocery shop and run errands…but other than that she was totally going to be a hermit from now on. People were not her thing. People were just terrible all around. And she'd had enough of terrible people.

She moved to the couch, wrapping herself up in a blanket. Darlene mused over what she would watch. Terrible shows about being tricked into online dating seemed like a good end to the night. It'd make her feel better at the very least.

Her cellphone rang loudly. Darlene jolted awake, startled. She wasn't used to her new ringtone. It used to be the theme song of an old cartoon she liked, but after everything went to hell she changed it to a normal ring in an effort to seem more adult. Now the ring was bleating loudly and annoying her. She looked at the front of the screen… her boss.

"Hello?"

"Hey, sorry, did I wake you?"

"No, Maria," Darlene lied. "What's up?"

"I had to fire Jacob. Can you cover his shift? You'd be working till three."

Darlene glanced at the clock to see it was a little past eight in the morning. "That's fine. I'll leave now."

She hopped in the shower, letting the warm water rush over her. She wasn't surprised that Maria had to fire Jacob. He was constantly late and unable to help any of the customers who came into the shop. The bookstore was small and dealt with books that couldn't be found at any of the chains. Business was slow, but the books were rare enough that Maria only needed to sell a few each month to keep the business going. Darlene liked how quiet it was and the fact that human interaction was minimal. She knew she needed to get over this slump she was in, but felt no desire to. Almost everything Darlene did as of late seemed to feed into it — her lifestyle, her job, even the stupid things she spent time watching and looking up online.

The bookstore was only a ten-minute drive to downtown and located between a coffee shop and a cheesy massage parlor. Maria hated the massage parlor. She thought it was tacky and ruined the charm of the street. Darlene usually liked to watch to see how many guys went in there. She swore it was a front for some hookers.

Darlene parked her car and headed toward the bookshop. She could already tell no one was in the store. She walked inside and waved to Maria.

"Oh, I am so glad you are here!" Maria exclaimed when she saw Darlene. "I'll have to hire someone right away, but you and I will have to work extra in the meantime."

"No problem," Darlene replied, shoving her purse under the front counter.

Darlene worked here for almost four years. Maria was a good boss. She always treated Darlene with respect and even gave her an entire month off after her father passed away three years ago. She was an older Native American woman with a bushy head of white hair that she barely cared enough to run a comb through. She wore large glasses that looked like they were from the seventies. Her fashion left a lot to be desired. Maria seemed to put on whatever she grabbed first and didn't look twice in the mirror afterward. For instance, today she had on a blue shirt with an off-color green skirt and black shoes. Her earrings were painted octopuses she had probably made herself — she liked making crazy jewelry.

"So," Darlene asked. "What happened with Jacob?"

Maria scowled. "He comes into work high as a kite, stinking of weed. Starts rambling to me about how he was in the woods last night and *like, totally felt something, like, man*," Maria said, mimicking Jacob's slow tone. "He was an hour late on top of it. I can't have someone late, stinking of weed and scaring off the few customers I get each month… especially after the last incident."

"Yeah, that was a mess." Jacob had hit on one of their regular clients in such a crass manner that she had threatened never to return again.

"Anyway, thank you so much for covering. I'm going to head off now. One of the grandkids is having a birthday party. You'll be okay?"

Darlene cast a sarcastic glance around the empty bookstore. "Wow, I hope I can handle it."

Maria laughed and grabbed her purse, heading to the door before stopping. "Hey, how was your date?"

Darlene frowned. "A total mess."

"Sorry, love. Hang in there, okay?" Maria said before leaving.

Hang in there. Darlene sighed. She has been hanging in there for way too long. When was she going to get a grip on her own life again? She walked around the shop to make sure everything was in its proper place. Darlene knew it would be, of course. It wasn't as if they had a ton of customers come through.

Maria had the marketable books up front, which brought in some tourist traffic during the summer. The farther back in the store one went, the stranger the books became. Darlene ended up in the back again, like she always did. Maria kept the supernatural books back here — books about ghosts, werewolves, mermaids and all sorts of paranormal creatures. Darlene always felt drawn to these; she never knew why. As a kid, she liked to pretend to be a ghost hunter. Nowadays, she liked to watch terrible B-movies about ghosts.

She trailed her fingers along the spines, letting the musty old-book smell wash over her. Darlene stopped in front of one book about ghosts, pulling it off the shelf. She had just flipped it open to a random page when the tiny bell on the door jingled. Surprised, Darlene looked up.

A tall man in amazing shape walked in. He had brown eyes, a beard and scruffy hair and wore a leather jacket. Darlene found herself gawking at him. He was so handsome her knees turned to jelly.

"Hi!" she said, but her voice sounded too high pitched, like she was eleven. "Hi, sorry, back here." She walked up front to him.

"Hello," he said in a deep voice that sent shivers down her back.

"Hi," Darlene repeated and then tried to get a hold of herself. "How can I help you?"

"I'm lost. I'm trying to find Roman's Tavern."

Her eyes widened. "I don't know if it's open yet."

Was this guy a hardcore alcoholic? It was still early in the morning, and he wanted to find a bar. Roman's Tavern was the only bar in town that Darlene hadn't ever gone to. It brought in a wild crowd that made her uneasy. Any time she drove past it and saw the crazy partying in there, she realized how much she wanted to go and that scared her. She was never much of a partier.

The fact that such an overwhelming urge to go when she drove by made her nervous. What if she went and lost her head?

The cops were there often, breaking up fights. Bike gangs were always seen there. Sometimes, if she left work at closing time, she'd drive by it and hear the thumping music and smell the cigarette smoke. She thought about going in every time. What would happen? Would she get hurt? What if she was missing out on something?

To Darlene, Roman's Tavern represented a life she could jump into if only she wasn't afraid. But she *was* too afraid. Life as a hermit was too comforting.

"Do you know where I can find it anyway?" he asked.

"It's down the street. On the corner, kind of pushed back a bit. It has this rundown broken sign that you might see if you drive by it."

"Thanks a lot, Miss…"

"Darlene." She held out her hand.

He stared at it for a second and then shook it. "Idris. Thanks for the help. You guys sell books about ghosts?" He pointed to the book she was holding when he came in.

His hand was so warm that Darlene had to snap herself back to the conversation. Was he sick? Shouldn't he be resting instead of going to some bar?

"Yes," she managed to respond. "We have a supernatural section in the back. Ghosts, vampires, werewolves…the usual."

"Werewolves, huh?" he replied. "Okay, well, nice to meet you."

Before Darlene could say anything else, he was gone.

She stood there, clutching her book to her chest, thinking about the feeling of warmth from his hand. What in the world was that about?

If you enjoyed this sample then look for **Alpha Packed: A BBW Paranormal Shifter Romance - Book 1**.

Here is a preview of **another story** you may also enjoy:

Alpha Feud: A BBW Paranormal Shifter Romance - Book 1

"Breaking news: A body has been found in the woods outside the town of Lancaster over the weekend. The county coroner has noted the cause to be what looks like an animal attack.

Sources say there have been sightings of 'wolf-like' creatures found in the area that may or may not be responsible, according to investigators. This is the third unsolved case of this nature that has been reported in the region."

ELIZA TUGGED at the zipper of her wind poncho in an attempt to cover her exposed skin. The wind was getting more fierce and it was still raining, but her network manager believed that rain added to the 'drama' of a broadcast. *Drama? What kind of 'drama' could there possibly be from covering a livestock contest?*

Of course, Eliza would never challenge her boss's choices to his face. Jim was a well-respected man in their town and, in fact, could be regarded as the biggest local celebrity. Jim used to work as an anchor in a major Los Angeles broadcasting station, but had chosen to return to Birkbridge and start his own broadcasting company. They had started off small but had managed to accumulate a decent following of loyal viewers and had therefore been able to expand into a full-fledged TV and radio station.

Under Jim's influence, Eliza had lived for a long time in a state of bedazzlement. After all, she had, once upon a time, fallen in love with the world of Jim's creation. Jim and his television station - Birkbridge NewsLine - had brought some sense of excitement to the otherwise boring little town. The problem was that, after five years of working for the man, she'd learned to see through the sparkly shades of spectacle. Once the illusion had shattered, the outcome was quite depressing; Eliza was, once more, living in the real world.

For people like Eliza's boyfriend, Andrew Freelander, 'normal' was not synonymous with boring. He was a man of simple pleasures and routine; he enjoyed his black coffee in the mornings and his beers in the evenings. Every other day, he went to shoot some pool at the local pub with his friends and colleagues from the weapons factory. Sometimes Eliza joined, sometimes she didn't. She didn't plan ahead most of the time, because she didn't want her entire life to be dominated by routine. Thanks to Jim, she felt as if her life might change for a while and become at least a little less monotonous. However, after many years, Eliza's new and 'exciting' life became its own routine.

And at the moment, she stood in front of a farm, reporting on an upcoming livestock show in the pouring rain. *Yippidy yay.*

"And now, reporting from the Birkbridge countryside farm: a soaked and very cold cow!" Eliza shouted into the camera.

Oliver, the cameraman, rolled his eyes. "Thank God we're not filming live television!" he yelled at her through the roaring wind. "And I don't see any cows around here, but I'm so bloody tired of not doing my job today that I might just be hallucinating!"

The wind was finally dying down and Oliver was pointing his camera at Eliza again. "None of that "cow" nonsense this time, Eliza! The people of this town are paying good money to get their news from a real human woman."

"You make a good point." Eliza smiled. Oliver was a good sport; he was the only British person in Birkbridge, and he certainly knew how to have a good bit of banter. Eliza decided to cut him some slack and snap into work mode; she knew that the rain might start again in a few seconds so they needed to get the shot right then and there.

"This is Eliza Zachary, reporting from the soon-to-be Birkbridge livestock fair. As you can see, preparations are under way for the upcoming festivities…"

Whenever she did stories like this, Eliza couldn't help but wonder what it would've been like if she'd accepted the job offer in Boston. The job had initially seemed way beyond her reach, but her father had pulled some strings with a few of his contacts at the news station and managed to convince Eliza to apply. To her amazement, she had been immediately accepted for the role of an on-site broadcasting journalist. Pursuing the job in Boston would have allowed Eliza to do what she'd always wanted and follow in the footsteps of her father. Granted, she wouldn't be on any real battlefront, but she would still be in the position to make history with her news stories. However, taking the job in Boston would also have prevented her from continuing her happy life with Andrew, her loving, loyal boyfriend.

Andrew and Eliza first met in their first year of college and had been inseparable ever since. She believed that Andrew was the only person, other than her dad, who she could truly be herself around. Although they didn't exactly have an instant connection, Eliza and Andrew grew close in a very natural way, and their relationship developed with ease. Before starting her first year of Media Studies, Eliza had promised herself that she would make an effort to interact with other people. College was meant to be the best time of her life, and Eliza wasn't about to let her insecurities get in the way of that. With some life coaching and advice from her dad and some styling tips from her mom, Eliza had fashioned her very own alter ego with which she would face the world head-on.

Through thick and thin, Eliza's father had always been her rock. Her mother, Jeanette, was always supportive, but she was sometimes a bit too fussy for Eliza to truly confide in her.

While growing up, Eliza had known her father as two men: the brave, effortlessly cool man who yelled over the sound of gunfire from the television screen, and the reserved, gentle man who tucked her into bed every night. Of course, the television Martin looked a lot different, since Eliza watched all his broadcasts as old recordings. By the time she was born, Martin had given up his career and settled down in Birkbridge to raise his family. He became a local historian, pursuing lengthy and in-depth projects relating to the foundational elements of Birkbridge life. These revolved around the three main industries in the town: coalmining, farming and manufacturing guns. His new book required him to research the inner workings of the Millstone Firearms factory, and he could often be found hanging out in the area, talking to some of the workers. Some of the workers didn't mind him, but others would sneer at him and ask him condescending questions. "Have you ever tried using Google, old man? You know we don't have all day to chat with you about your picture books."

Despite his seemingly old-fashioned methods and even though he was a bit of a social outcast, Martin was still unbelievably charming. Perhaps it was due to his immaculately well-preserved good looks, or maybe because of his patience and open-minded listening skills, but Martin's investigative projects usually bore fantastic results. He often took on paid projects for some extra cash. Sometimes, locals would hire him to investigate and produce their family trees. In other cases, his clients were people who wanted him to find anecdotes or even write entire biographies for their

dead relatives' funerals. One thing was for sure; his
clients were never disappointed.

Going along with her father's suggestion, Eliza
joined the drama club and after five months, Eliza had
had a decent amount of interaction with the club's one
and only groupie; a cute senior named Andrew. At first,
she was a little annoyed with his tendency to hang
around and watch their practices. Eliza was new to this
scene and still felt a bit self-conscious, particularly
around people who weren't even part of the theater
group. For this reason, Andrew's casual presence had
frustrated her a little bit. Who was this guy? Didn't he
have anything better to do?

The first time that Eliza found herself alone with
Andrew, she had been unexpectedly upfront with him.
She was usually shy around guys, but she found him so
annoying that her frustration managed to surpass her
bashfulness. Although sarcasm hadn't been part of her
repertoire at the time, Eliza's first conversation with
Andrew was loaded with it.

"Haven't seen you in a while," she'd said with a
cheeky grin on her face. "You must've been really busy
lately."

Andrew had been at their practices every single day
that week, so he laughed at her ironic insinuations that
he had no life. And, as it turned out, Andrew had liked
Eliza's direct approach to conversation. Due to her
former friendlessness, Eliza hadn't really learned how
to engage in small talk and empty chitchat; she was an

all-or-nothing kind of girl. Andrew, as an attractive college senior, had become accustomed to empty, flirtatious interactions with the opposite sex. However, Andrew was a self-proclaimed monogamist and he quickly tired of the attention overload. Throughout college, he'd been looking to settle down, but to his dismay, all the co-eds seemed the same to him; he never found anyone amongst his groupies who really challenged him the right way. So Andrew became a groupie himself and started hanging out with the drama club. As he explained to Eliza, he was looking to find some truth in the fiction of theater. Eliza had rolled her eyes and called him a cheeseball. Then they exchanged looks, Eliza's mouth twisting into a crooked smile, and they both burst into laughter.

Andrew had been persistent, and had won Eliza over within two weeks. They'd hang out after the theater club practices, and their private meetings had escalated. At first, they met up in cafés, then bars, and eventually, Andrew's apartment. Quickly, Eliza and Andrew became in sync with one another, and there was no awkwardness in discussing their plans for the future. After she completed her sophomore year, Andrew asked Eliza to move in with him, and she gladly accepted.

Andrew had graduated three years earlier than Eliza and immediately got a job at Millstone Firearms. After five years his responsibilities had increased immensely. Despite his reputation for being late to almost everything, Andrew was nothing but exceptional at what he did, in fact, ever since Andrew received his promotion to junior head of sales, Millstone Firearms had managed to out-sell their competitors by ten percent annually, which meant that they were finally on their way to becoming the most successful firearms manufacturer in the country.

For Eliza, parting with Andrew hadn't really been an option. Since she hadn't, in her wildest dreams, expected that the Boston network would actually consider her application, let alone offer her a job, Eliza had been completely befuddled about how to act when she'd received the offer. Deep down, she had already known that Andrew would not be willing to give up his job and leave Birkbridge, and she also realized that he simply wouldn't be able to keep up with the pace of life in the east coast. After all, the only things that kept Andrew's absent-mindedness at bay were his routines and habits, but he was completely unable to adjust to changes in his schedule.

Nevertheless, Eliza had had a tiny speckle of hope when she confronted Andrew about her job offer. He had been incredibly sweet, kissing Eliza and telling her that he was so proud of her; after all, what were the odds for getting such an incredible job offer straight-out-of-college? However, the fantasy wasn't meant to last. After lengthy conversations over breakfast, dinner and weekend pillow talk, Andrew and Eliza eventually came to the sad yet inevitable conclusion that the move to Boston wasn't going to pan out. They both knew that Andrew had worked incredibly hard to achieve his current company status, and neither of them believed that he should have to start from square one again. They discussed the possibility of Eliza moving on her own, but her fully packed Boston work schedule would ultimately overrule the possibility of her flying out to see Andrew once every few months. For Andrew, given his recent promotion, the chances of taking time for visitation days were also very slim.

As Eliza helped Oliver pack up his camera equipment, she told herself that she had no regrets. In actuality, the decision to stay in Birkbridge with Andrew had been a no-brainer. She had been able to get everything she wanted: a loving boyfriend *and* a job. Granted, this job may not have been a first choice, but it was certainly not a job that anyone in their right mind could complain about.

Arriving home, Eliza checked the time on her phone, 6:29 pm, and in the process discovered several texts from Melissa, one of her three best friends and also, coincidentally, a cousin.

5:30: *Done with work, where are you right now?*

5:44: *Not gonna bother going home first, brought a change of clothes to work so heading to the bar now! Will see you there.*

6:08: *There's a hot guy here. Hurry or I'll go home with him!*

6:10: *Just kidding but seriously, get here already.*

When Eliza walked into *Nelly's*, Melissa was sitting at their usual spot. There were a few empty glasses already lined up at the table, but she was still looking relatively sharp. As Eliza knew from experience,

Melissa could be trusted to hold her liquor. Even on nights when she consumed triple the doses of her friends, Melissa would always be the last one standing.

Eliza took a seat opposite her friend. "So where's this dreamy guy? I was almost expecting you to be gone by the time I arrived."

"All kidding aside, if my vodka-goggles aren't deceiving me, I think there really *is* a somewhat hot guy here tonight. He's at the bar though, so be a doll and check him out for me while you're up there?"

Eliza rolled her eyes and sighed dramatically, but she couldn't stop herself from smiling. "Oh, all right then. But only because I love you."

"You're the best!" Melissa beamed, giving her friend an overly exaggerated wink. There was something about their weekly girly meet-ups that had spurred the friends to engage in a satirical 80's-housewife-routine.

Eliza came back from the bar, carrying two cocktails. "So, no sight of Brienne yet. Or has she also wondered off with some mystery man?"

"Yes. She's finally left boring old Tom and those dreadful kids and found herself a real man," Melissa responded, without breaking character.

At that moment, Brienne came through the door, dithering about as always. She wiped her feet on the carpet and, spotting the flaw of their seating arrangement, shuffled over to another table and grabbed a chair.

"Hey, sorry I'm so late, what did I miss?"

"Not much. Well, Melissa has spotted someone she thinks is hot, but that's about it," Eliza responded matter-of-factly.

"Ah, good, so I didn't miss anything," Brienne confirmed, slouching back on her chair and looking calm at last.

If you enjoyed this sample then look for **Alpha Feud: A BBW Paranormal Shifter Romance - Book 1**.

Here is a preview of **another story** you may also enjoy:

Star Bright, Book 1 by Carla Coxwell

THE SUNLIGHT creeps into my room. I groan and turn my head the other direction, trying to sleep through it. The last thing I feel like doing is getting up this morning. I never want to get up again. Everything I've done for the last few months has been robotic.

The holiday season is usually my favorite time of year. There is nothing I love more than browsing around the shops, looking for the best things to buy for my parents and friends.

That was before everything in my life went to hell. Now the thought of seeing anyone or even shopping makes me want to go back to sleep for the rest of the day.

Maggie… my daughter…

This would have been her first Christmas.

The thought comes to me quickly, before I can attempt to stop it. I try to stop all thoughts of her. Yet all it does is drive me into the pit of despair even faster. If I start thinking about her now, I will never get out of bed. I tell myself I will handle this morning the way I handle every other morning – with baby steps.

Open my eyes. It sounds ridiculous to make that a step but when I tell myself baby steps, I truly mean baby steps. If I think of what to do all at once – get up, shower, make coffee – it is all so overwhelming that I don't want to leave my bed.

The baby steps continue. Get out of bed. Walk to the bathroom. Brush my teeth. Open the shower door. Depression makes even the thought of getting in the shower to wash, only to do it all over again tomorrow, seem idiotic.

After my shower, I decide to go grocery shopping. I remember coming home last night and not finding anything substantial to eat. Instead I ate three slices of bread and went to bed. My stomach is growling loudly at me, demanding something decent to eat.

I slip on an oversized long-sleeved T-shirt and a pair of baggy jeans. Gone are the times when I cared about what I looked like. I don't want anyone to notice me ever again. It is safe to be by myself. I tell myself I can handle being alone.

Before I leave, I check my bank account on my phone. My savings are dwindling. I need to get a job. This can't last forever. When I quit my job, I figured something else would fall into my lap. But it's hard to have things fall in your lap when you never leave your bed. *I'm becoming pathetic.* I grab my purse and head out into the chilly morning.

A thin layer of snow covers the ground. The sun has now retreated behind a mass of gray clouds. They threaten a heavy snowfall. I wouldn't mind if it snowed everyone in. Sadly, Netflix is my new best friend.

The grocery store is brimming with families with their kids in tow, out of school for the holidays. I curse myself for not thinking of this before I left my apartment this morning. I wander around blindly, my list in hand, as my gaze falls on the kids around me. My heart beats quickly in my chest and my skin feels numb. All I want is to take Maggie's hand and walk through the store with her. I would kill to see her try to grab something off the shelf or plead with me to get her a doll in the small toy section.

Instead I am alone, a panic attack blooming on the brink. What is my trigger exactly? Happy kids? Couples who look down at their children and beam? I feel stupid as I park my basket in a random aisle and bolt into the restroom, which is thankfully empty. I go into one of the stalls then close my eyes tightly.

I can't live like this forever. Every time I decide to leave the house, I find myself overwhelmed by people or past memories. Everything seems to be trying to get my attention, telling me that my old dreams have died and I am letting life pass me by.

I have done things in my life that I am not proud of. I have terrible taste in men. I have a habit of only being attracted to assholes or drunks and I have had no issues cheating on people to be with someone else.

My skin feels hot and itchy as I try to avoid the panic attack that will knock me over. I focus on my breathing.

I am here. I am here. I am here.

I am nowhere else. What I have done in the past is in the past. I can't get Maggie back. I won't get Paul back after what I've done to him. I even feel like I deserve what Robbs has done to me.

Focusing on my breathing and repeating my mantra helps slow my heart rate down. I am glad no one else has come into the bathroom. The last thing I need is someone else thinking I am crazy.

After ten minutes, I am able to leave the stall. I splash some water on my face and look in the mirror. I hardly recognize myself. I have let myself go. I have to get a handle on my life but I have no idea how to do so. I have been hoping a sign will come to let me know what to do next. But what if that is just an excuse to give myself a pass on my shitty behavior? What if this is the sign – almost having a panic attack in a supermarket over happy children?

I leave the restroom, ready to get my grocery shopping done without further incident. By the time I leave the supermarket, I am feeling grounded again. Sometimes my head gets the best of me. I decide I'll brush it from my mind and go get a coffee. I haven't bought anything frozen, so I don't need to get home right away. My inner chef refuses to die, so the thought of making a frozen meal still does not appeal to me, even with how depressed I am.

It has been a while since I have treated myself to an overpriced iced coffee. But today is quickly becoming a day that is unlike the others so I head into the coffee shop, trying to ignore the small crowd standing in line to wait. I find myself lost in thought at the menu, which seems to have doubled in items since the last time I was here.

Someone taps on my shoulder, and I nearly jump out of my skin. I take a deep breath and turn around, fearing who it will be.

If you enjoyed this sample then look for **Star Bright, Book 1 by Carla Coxwell**.

Other Books by Darla Dunbar

- The Romeo Alpha BBW Paranormal Shifter Romance Series (This series precedes the "Romeo Alpha Blood Lines Romance Series")

- The Alpha Feud BBW Paranormal Shifter Romance Series

- The Alpha Packed BBW Paranormal Shifter Romance Series

- The Daemon Paranormal Romance Chronicles

- The Mind Talker Paranormal Romance Series

- The Leather Satchel Paranormal Romance Series

Get the latest update on new releases from the author at:

https://darladunbar.com/newsletter/

About the Author - Darla Dunbar

Darla has been interested in paranormal romance since she was a teenager in high school. It was then that she discovered she could fulfill her fantasies through her writing.

Observing people and human behavior in the area of romance has always been one of her favorite pastimes. Combining that with an overactive imagination is a sure fire way of coming up with interesting themes.

Connect with Darla Dunbar

I really appreciate you reading my book! Here are my social media coordinates:

Friend me on Facebook:
https://www.facebook.com/darladunbar/

Follow me on Twitter: https://twitter.com/DarlDunbar

Check me out on Goodreads:
https://www.goodreads.com/author/show/8425857.Darla_Dunbar

Subscribe to my newsletter:
https://darladunbar.com/newsletter/

Visit my website: https://darladunbar.com/

www.ingramcontent.com/pod-product-compliance
Lightning Source LLC
Chambersburg PA
CBHW030754200726
48288CB00004B/1170